THE YOUNG Gangsters

THE YOUNG Gangsters

E J P
Murphy

JB
JOHN BLAKE

Published by John Blake Publishing Ltd, 3 Bramber Court,
2 Bramber Road, London W14 9PB, England

First published in 2002

ISBN 1 904034 39 X

British Library Cataloguing-in-Publication Data: A catalogue record
for this book is available from the British Library.

Design by ENVY

Printed and bound in Great Britain by CPD (Wales)

1 3 5 7 9 10 8 6 4 2

Papers used by John Blake Publishing Ltd are natural, recyclable products
made from wood grown in sustainable forests. The manufacturing processes
conform to the environmental regulations of the country of origin.

contents

prologue

THEY STOOD INSIDE THE SHOP, ONE GUARDING THE DOOR, THE REST MILLING AROUND THE COUNTER. EIGHT OF THEM, ALL WEARING THE SAME CLOTHES – JEANS, SWEATSHIRTS, WHITE PUMPS AND LONG BLACK COATS HANGING DOWN TO THEIR ANKLES. ON THEIR HEADS THEY WORE BASEBALL CAPS WITH THE MONOGRAM 'TYG' ON THE PEAK, SHORT FOR 'THE YOUNG GANGSTERS'.

The one who was talking was called Jimmy 'The Feet' Day. The 'Feet' because he loved dancing. He said to the shopkeeper,

"Now... mister, I ain't going to tell you again, 20 quid a day or we're going to ruin your stock. You ever smelt petrol when it's doused all around you?" Jimmy looked to his left and spoke to the person beside him. "Right, Dave, douse the counter first, then the store room, then him."

"No, no, please." The shopkeeper grabbed his arm."I'll pay, please don't; you'll ruin me. Please, please."

Dave looked at his leader. Jimmy nodded, "OK, mister." He looked at the owner again. "140 a week, 100 up front, right?"

"OK, OK, I'll pay, I'll pay," the owner replied. He ran around the counter, opened the till, took out £100 and passed it over to Jimmy.

Jimmy counted it, put it in his pocket and said to the owner, "You miss one week and we'll be back … try to go to the police and we'll burn your house down with your family in it. Got it?"

The owner looked at him, now really frightened. "You'll get your money."

"Yeah," Jimmy said to him, reading his thoughts. "We know where you live, we'll be watching all the time, remember that. Let's go boys."

Jimmy moved to the door. Opening it, he looked back at the the owner. "One of my boys will come to see you every Friday night; don't let me down, and remember," he put his finger to his lips, "not a word."

Jimmy walked out of the door followed by the rest of the gang. Outside, they walked down the pavement, four abreast, pushing past people. They were noticeable in their long black coats and caps, but much more noticeable were their young faces.

Jimmy was the eldest, he was 16. The youngest, Sammy 'Bellows' Jones was only 14. His nickname 'Bellows' was because he was always farting. Dave 'Mack the Knife' Smith, was also 16 – he always carried a knife and used it a lot. Paul 'Gummy' White, 15, lost his teeth in a punch-up when he got hit with a baseball bat. Micky 'The Ferret' Taret, 15, could get into any window, hence the nickname. Bertie 'Knuckles' Cooney, 16, could fight like any fully grown six-footer. He worshipped Jimmy and would do anything for him and did. Jackie Sweeney 'Todd', 14, loved trouble and hated school with a vengeance – he never went. Paul 'Looney Tunes' Higgins, 14, was mad as a hatter; would do anything for the gang.

These were the young gangsters – terrifying, cold-blooded. They terrified their neighbourhood and those beyond. Some people said they were only kids and would grow out of it. Little did they know the power of friendship and what they would do for it.

This is the story of eight mates who didn't care for anyone but each other. A story of hate, lust, robbery and power.

Eight boys from the slums – it could only end one way.

Chapter 1

JIMMY DAY SAT IN THE LIVING ROOM, FEET UP ON THE SETTEE, A CAN OF BEER IN ONE HAND, A CIGARETTE IN THE OTHER, MUSIC BLARING FROM HIS CD EARPHONES WHICH WERE HUNG AROUND HIS NECK. HIS DAD, TRYING TO TELL HIM SOMETHING, WALKED OVER AND SWITCHED OFF HIS CD.

Jimmy jumped up, startled. "What you bloody doing?" He looked at his dad, hate in his eyes. "Don't touch my stuff, you hear me?"

"I hear you, you dumb shit. I've been trying to speak to you for five bloody minutes."

"What do you bloody want then?" he snarled standing up, facing his dad, eyes blazing. "More fucking money, you lazy bastard? You want to get out and get a bloody job."

"Don't talk to me like that," his dad shouted back at him.

"I'm your bloody dad." He stepped nearer to Jimmy. "I ought to give you this," he said, putting his fist up.

"Yeah, you wish," Jimmy said, pushing past him. He walked over to the window, looking out across the big estate. "God, what a dump," he said to himself.

The estate he lived on was in the heart of Camden. The high-rise flats he lived in were amongst the worst in London, neglected by the local council.

He looked through the nicotine-stained glass windows down on to the play areas. He laughed aloud. "Play areas," he murmured, "bloody slum-infested areas".

Across the way he could see the City and, looming in the background, the NatWest Tower dominated the skyline. He kicked the wall below the window. "All that fucking money spent on that crap, it would have been better to spend it on this bloody estate or something decent like homes for the homeless, hospitals, etc. Bloody nerve."

Below he could see his mate Bertie's flat, 14 floors down in the identical block opposite. Bertie's mum was hanging out the washing on her balcony. Jimmy missed the smell of washing. He remembered his mum used to wash the clothes and linen every day. That's one of the things he missed about his mum since she'd died.

Kathleen Day? She died aged 44. They said it was cancer but Jimmy blamed his dad. Jimmy was only 11 years old when she died, but he remembered his dad beating her up when he came home drunk on Saturday and Sunday afternoons and nights.

"I'll have him one day, Mum," he said as he stood over her grave as they lowered her body down. His older sister Alice gripped his hand. Mark, his younger brother, held his other hand. Mark was two years younger than him.

His dad, half-pissed, looked down into the grave. "I'll look after them, Kathleen," he said out loud for the benefit of the mourners.

"You won't bloody look after me," he heard his sister say to herself. "I'm off out of it." And she went all right. 16 years old at the time, but she got through OK.

"You lend me some money then?"

His dad's voice brought him back to reality. Jimmy, still looking out of the window, put his hand in the back pocket of his jeans and pulled out a wad of notes. He peeled away a £20 note and threw it across the room without looking at him.

"That's £80 you owe me, don't forget."

"I'll give it back to you one day, don't worry about that," his dad said to Jimmy's back.

Jimmy turned away from the window and looked straight at his dad. He spoke with hate in his voice. "I never worry about anything or anybody."

Jimmy looked at his watch. It was just after 7.40am. He hadn't been to bed yet, but then he wasn't tired. He looked at his dad again and said, "Get Mark up, he'll be late for school."

"He's up, having his breakfast. What a fine example you are, his big brother who ain't been to school for two bloody years."

"Yeah, I know," Jimmy said. "I left because you're always pissed, never bringing any money in the bloody house. Someone had to. You drove my sister away, but someone had to take care of Mark, and I am, so shut up."

Jimmy walked past him and into the kitchen. His brother

was sitting there reading a football magazine and munching a bacon sandwich.

"Hello, bruv." Mark looked at his brother, admiration in his eyes. "Late in again last night," he smiled. "Was she nice?" Giggling, he went back to his magazine.

"Cheeky sod," Jimmy said ruffling his brother's hair. "Want to come with me and the boys tonight. We're off down the Camden Palace dancing. It's Friday and you're 14 tomorrow. Call it an early treat. What do you say?"

"Thanks, bruv. Do I get to wear the gear you wear?"

"No bloody chance, we're going dancing and that's it. No fighting or anything else tonight," Jimmy said pouring himself a coffee and lighting a fag. "Finish your sarnie and I'll walk to school with you. I've got to meet Bertie and Dave downstairs at 8.30."

"I'm ready, Jimmy, I'll just get my coat." Mark pushed his chair back, stood up, put the rest of the sarnie in his mouth and walked out into the hallway. A minute later, he called out: "Ready, Jimmy."

The lift, as usual, was broken. Jimmy opened the door to the stairwell. Mark pushed in front of him and started to walk down the stairs. It was cold and damp, there was graffiti everywhere.

"God, what a shit-heap," Jimmy said to himself. "I'd like to get them councillors and make them live in this squalor, see how they like it."

They reached the bottom of the stairwell and pushed out into the fresh air; well, air anyway. Dave and Bertie were waiting on the other side of the green.

"Hiya, Mark," Dave said to Jimmy's brother, "going to school?"

"Watcha, young 'un," Bertie said to him. He looked over to Jimmy. "Hello, pal, walking to school with him?"

"Yeah, Bert. Come on, let's go. Got to see that gay bloke's shop today, might bring in some extra dough. We're meeting the others over in Regent's Park at 10. Come on, let's get Mark to school."

They left Mark at his school in Camden Town and then walked over to Regent's Park. The sun was just coming out as they entered the park by the entrance at the top of Parkway. Jimmy had told the rest of his young gang to meet at the back of the zoo. They were all there – none of them went to school. They were either expelled or just didn't turn up.

Paul White saw them coming across the park. "Here they come, dead on time." He looked at his watch, it was 10.05am.

Jimmy walked over to them, Dave and Bertie either side of him, as if protecting him.

"Whatcha, mates," he said, nodding at each of them.

Pete Higgins looked at him. "Morning, Jimmy, Dave, Bertie. We're all ready for action."

"Yeah, let's go," young Sammy shouted.

"Hold on, hold on!" Jimmy looked round the group, all of them looking at him as if he was God. "We've got a bit of planning to do here first. Now come on, let's sit on the grass. I can outline it better for you then."

They all followed Jimmy out on to the grass away from the zoo. Sitting down in a circle, they looked like a bunch of Red Indians ready to have a pow-wow.

"Right." He looked around at them, knowing that they would listen to every word he said. "The shop is over in St John's Wood High Street. It's not a Paki shop, it's a boutique, run by a gay guy. He looks vulnerable to blackmail. Anyway, this is what we're going to do. Pete, you've got a nice baby face. When you go in there, you tell the gay guy you're looking for a present for your sister. Lead him on, then when he gets friendly, give a shout. I'll be outside the window."

"Hold on, Jimmy." Pete looked at him startled. "I hate these bleeding poofs, I might stick one on him if he starts on me."

"Well don't, you'll ruin everything. Just do as I say," Jimmy told him. He put his hand on Pete's shoulder. "Don't worry, mate, we'll be right outside. Come on then, let's go."

They all got up, brushing the bits of leaves and grass off their coats and walked towards the park's exit, just off the Outer Circle.

Pete walked over to Jimmy. "Here, you can't be serious, Jimmy, it'll never work, will it?"

Jimmy looked down at him and smiled. "It'll work," he said. "I've put a lot of work in on this one."

"The guy's name is Harry Pearson, he's as bent as Quasimodo. A bloke I know in Kentish Town said he's always chasing the fellas, been inside a couple of times for it, so he'll pay up, believe me. He doesn't want to go back inside, even though it's a queers' paradise in the nick. Anyway, you'll be OK Pete, never let you down yet, have I?"

"Yeah, yeah, I'll do it. What's he going to do anyway?" Pete looked around at the others, waiting for a reply, but none came.

They crossed Prince Albert Road and into St John's Wood High Street. Jimmy stopped them on the corner.

"Right - Paul, Sammy, Jackie, you go in with Bertie. There's a coffee bar opposite the shop. You wait in there until I buzz, yeah? The rest of you come with me. Bertie, take your lot first. I'll see you later."

Bertie walked off. Jimmy waited till they were at the entrance to the coffee bar, then turned to the others.

"Come on, let's go. Pete, I'll come in the shop ten minutes after you, pretend I'm looking for something, or better still, shout out and I'll come on in then. When you see me come in, shout out loud, 'You can fucking cut that out mate,' then I'll come over and confront him, OK?"

"Well yeah, OK, Jimmy, but don't let me down."

They walked up the high street, Pete ahead of them. He stopped at the shop, looked in the window, moved to the door, pushed it open and walked in.

"Let's go," Jimmy said to the remainder of the gang. "Now, when I go into the shop, you lot go over to the café, get a Coke or something and wait. Keep your eye on the shop door, the notice saying "Open" or "Closed", when I've challenged the queer guy."

"My dad used to call them ginger beers," Micky said, interrupting.

"Shut up, Micky and bloody listen. As I was saying ..." Jimmy glared at Micky.

"Sorry," Micky murmured.

"Keep your eyes on the door. When you see the "Closed" sign, come on over. Tell Paul and Sammy to stay outside, keep watch, know what I mean? You come in, right?"

"Right, Jimmy," they all answered together.

As they drew nearer to the shop Dave and Micky crossed the road and walked up to the café, looked at Jimmy, waved and then disappeared inside.

"What a couple of plonkers," Jimmy said to himself. He stopped outside the shop, looked through the window, squinted his eyes, looking left and right. He could just see Pete talking to Harry Pearson.

Even though Pete didn't look at the window, Jimmy knew he'd seen him. Jimmy nodded his head. Pete reacted right away as Jimmy walked through the doorway. Pete pushed Harry Pearson away from him.

"You dirty pervert, keep your fucking hands off me."

Jimmy rushed over. He grabbed hold of Pearson. "I saw that, you dirty bastard. You tried to grab his cock... I'm going to tell the police."

"No, no please, I didn't. He's trying it on. I never went near him."

Pete looked at him. "You tried to grab my privates, you bastard. I'm going to have you for this. Call the police, Jimmy."

Harry stopped dead. "Hang on," he said, "you're in this together, you're setting me up."

Jimmy ignored him, walked over to the door and turned the 'Open' sign to 'Closed'. He turned round facing Harry Pearson. "Yeah, that's right, Harry, I know all about you."

The door opened and the rest of the gang, except Bernie and Dave, walked in.

"Hey, what's this?" Harry was getting frightened now. "Please don't hurt me." He backed away from Jimmy.

"We ain't going to hurt you, Harry, as long as you co-operate, know what I mean?"

"What do you want?" Harry looked from one to the other. "If you're not going to beat me up, then..."

"Well Harry, this is how it is. I'll keep it quiet 'cause I know that if the cops come, you'll spin off down to the nick and you could go down for a three stretch. If my mate here says you assaulted him, and he will, you'll lose the shop and..."

"How much do you want? It is money you want, isn't it?" Harry said looking at Jimmy. Going to blackmail me, are you?"

Jimmy looked at him, a nasty look coming into his eyes. "100 quid a week," he said. "You take it in this shop, you must make thousands. Yes or no? Make your mind up. Don't forget, if this gets out, you're ruined, remember that."

"You bastards." He looked at them one by one. "I'm bowing down to a bunch of bloody kids. OK, I'll pay you."

Jimmy looked at him. "I'll take 100 up front. One of us will pick up the money weekly on a Saturday morning. You are open Saturdays, Harry?"

"Yes I am." Harry walked over to the counter, went round the back of it, and passed two £50 notes over to Jimmy.

"Here's your blood money, now get out of my shop."

"Come on boys, let's go." Jimmy winked at Harry. "Thanks, see you next Saturday."

Jimmy walked to the door, opened it, let the others out, turned round to Harry and said, "Go straight Harry, it doesn't pay to be gay," and walked out of the shop after turning the sign back to 'Open' on the door.

Back outside, Jimmy and his gang walked back to the park.

"OK, boys, I've got to go now but see you all down at the pub tonight, OK?"

They all nodded.

"Thanks, Jimmy," Pete said, "it worked out like you said it would."

"Oh, by the way, I'm bringing my kid brother tonight. It's his birthday tomorrow. Right. . . see you later."

"Come on, Dave, Bert, let's drum up some more work and get ready for tonight. See you later boys."

Chapter 2

JIMMY DAY WAS BORN IN HACKNEY TO AN IRISH MOTHER, KATHLEEN. BESIDES JIMMY, SHE ALSO HAD A DAUGHTER, ALICE. WHEN JIMMY WAS BORN, ALICE WAS NEARLY FIVE. HIS DAD, BILLY DAY, WAS TEN YEARS OLDER THAN JIMMY'S MOTHER. HE WAS A LABOURER ON ANY BUILDING SITE THAT WOULD EMPLOY HIM; HE WAS A LAZY BASTARD, ALWAYS DRUNK AND NEVER HAD MONEY IN HIS POCKETS. HE STOLE HIS WIFE'S MONEY, WHO (POOR SOUL) WORKED AT FOUR JOBS, CLEANING OFFICES AND HOUSES EARLY MORNING UNTIL LATE. SHE LEFT THE KIDS WITH HER MATE, MARY, WHO LIVED TWO DOORS AWAY. SOME SAY BILLY, JIMMY'S DAD, WAS KNOCKING MARY OFF.

They had lived in a two-room apartment in a block of flats off Mare Street, Hackney. It wasn't too bad; Jimmy's mum kept it spotless, and like most Irish mums, she took pride in her home. Kathleen Day was a lovely woman. She came over from Ireland when she was 17, but as Jimmy once said to his sister, "out of sheer bad luck she met Billy Day". He got her pregnant; the rest is history.

Two years after Jimmy's birth, Mark was born. After his mum's death the young family were left with a drunken arsehole of a father.

He soon got them into debt, leaving the bills, rent and everything else unpaid. They were finally evicted and sent to a badly run-down estate in Camden Town.

There was virtually nothing coming into the house, so Jimmy, who was by then 12, started to steal from shops or anywhere he could get money from. His sister, Alice, was doing a paper round to help, Social Services paid the rent but most of the food money they gave Jimmy's dad was spent on booze or women. Over the next few years, Jimmy started to loathe his dad, and his only thoughts were for his brother and sister.

Jimmy started to stay out late, even though he was then only 14. He also started to drink and smoke, having formed his own gang of kids who lived around the area.

At night, they used to go down the West End snatching handbags, and stealing from shops and stores. While watching a film one night at his mate's house, Bertie Cooney's, he got the idea of wearing long coats and baseball hats and forming a proper gang. A protection racket was his first idea; going into vulnerable shops run by Asians and people who couldn't fight back. It was to prove a great money-maker.

Alice left home just after her mum died and was now married with a baby boy, but Jimmy never saw much of her, as she lived in Manchester. He phoned her up once in a while, but she never came down to London.

* * *

Jimmy was in the bathroom getting ready to go dancing with his mates and his brother Mark. Bertie and Dave had come back to his flat and had a drink. At 5pm they had gone home to get changed. Before they left, Jimmy handed Dave five envelopes. "Here, give these to Bertie and the boys, bit extra for you and Bertie, OK? Had quite a good week." He smiled.

"Thanks, Jimmy, going to get me a nice sweat with that, I'll see you at the pub later!"

Jimmy looked at himself in the full-length mirror. He was tall for his age, just over 6ft and quite heavy, 11st in weight, pretty fast on his feet, good with his fists, but better with the cut-down baseball bat he carried up his sleeve, held there with a strong elastic band. He was also handsome, with very dark hair and blue eyes. "You've got Mum's good looks," his sister had said to him once. Jimmy knew he was handsome and used his looks to snare the girls. They were always flocking around him and he loved it.

Tonight he had donned a pair of Ralph Lauren jeans and light T-shirt, new Reeboks, and a dark cotton jacket.

"Snazzy," he said to himself, combing back his short dark hair.

"Jimmy," his brother's voice broke the silence.

"Yeah, Mark," he shouted back.

"Can I borrow your Reebok sweatshirt, just for tonight?"

"OK, but just tonight, and hurry up, it's nearly 8.00, time to meet the rest of the boys down the pub."

It was just after 8.30pm when Jimmy and Mark walked into the Nag's Head just off Camden High Street. It was packed to the rafters.

The landlord turned a blind eye to the young ones who drank in his pub; they brought good money in, and he didn't want to lose it.

"Let's get around the bar, bruv," he said to Mark. "I think the boys should be over there."

"Jimmy! Hey! Over here," a voice boomed over the noise in the bar.

"Over there, Jimmy," his brother said to him, "It's Micky the Ferret."

They pushed their way way over to the corner of the bar. Micky was standing on a chair.

"Here, Jimmy, Mark," he kept waving to them.

"For Christ's sake, I wish he'd shut up," Jimmy said to his brother, as they reached Micky and the rest of the boys.

Paul stood up as they came across. "Here, Jimmy, have my seat."

"Na, na, you're all right, mate," Jimmy shouted to him above the noise. "I've got me new Ralphs on, don't want to crease them, know what I mean? Thanks anyway."

Dave was sat next to his girlfriend, Jenny. She was only 15 but drank and smoked like a trooper, and other things, too.

"Whatcha, Jimmy," she said to him, eyes sparkling, "See you have your little brother with you tonight."

Jimmy looked at her, smiling. "Yeah, it's his fourteenth birthday tomorrow. Me and the boys sorta taking him out 'celebrating', know what I mean?"

"Gotcha," she replied.

Jimmy knew she was half-pissed and left it at that. He looked across at Bertie and nodded his head for him to come over. Bertie stood up, picked his drink up and walked over to him. Bertie whistled, "You look smart, mate, got a date?"

Jimmy smiled. "Not really, I'll most probably pull a bird inside the club. Anyway, the night's young yet, let's have a drink anyway, and get the boys over here. I want to have a word."

They were all gathered around Jimmy near the bar, each of them had a drink in their hand.

"Listen, I want no trouble tonight, OK? It's my kid brother's birthday treat, so let's put business and fighting aside, unless we're provoked, then we'll go in and sort it."

"Yeah, sure, Jimmy. We won't spoil it for him, don't worry. . . will we, lads?" Paul said looking around at the others.

"Not likely," piped up Jackie Sweeney.

"No way, Jimmy," shouted Dave, who was at the bar buying more drinks. The others all agreed with him and the night went on.

It was just after 12.30am and people were coming out on to the streets from the clubs. Jimmy and his pals came out from the Palais, most of them with girls, except Mark, Jimmy's brother and Pete Higgins.

"Listen, Pete, take Mark home will ya, for me? I've got to take this bird home." The girl he was with was about 20, but as Jimmy said, "Age don't matter, they're all the same laying down, and if they're ugly, well, you don't look at the mantelpiece when you poke the fire."

"OK, Jimmy," Pete said to him. "I'll see you tomorrow. Come on, Mark."

"I'll see you later, Mark," Jimmy said to his brother. "Won't be late. Did you have a good time?"

"Thanks, bruv, it was great," said Mark as he walked away with Pete.

Jimmy shouted after him, "Look under the bed when you get home, Mark, and Happy Birthday."

Jimmy turned to the girl he was with and said, "I've got him a new tracksuit and a Ralph Lauren jacket, you know. Come on, I'll take you home."

Chapter 3

BERTIE COONEY KICKED THE BEDCLOTHES OFF HIS BODY, SAT UP IN BED AND STRETCHED. HE LOOKED AT THE CEILING, SHOOK HIS HEAD AND JUMPED OUT OF BED.

He looked at the clock on his bedside table; it was a little after 10am, Monday morning. He walked over to the bedroom window, he pulled the curtain back and peered out; it was cloudy. It felt warm, but it looked like rain. He craned his head so he could look up at the tower block opposite. Jimmy usually leaned over his balcony this time of the morning, but Bertie couldn't see him today.

"I'll nip over and see him later," he murmured to himself.

Bertie was just past his sixteenth birthday. Born in County Mayo in Ireland, his father couldn't find work so he packed up his family (five kids) and moved to London, where they lived with Bertie's uncle in Willesden.

His dad, Brogan Cooney, soon found work, on building sites. After three years, they were given a council flat in Camden; that's where Bertie had found his mate, Jimmy Day. They had met at the local Catholic school. Jimmy had been in a fight with another boy and, when Jimmy was winning, the boy's mates had joined in. Bertie had seen it, and joined in to help Jimmy. They'd become close ever since.

"That boy will get you in a load of trouble," his dad had told him after he met Jimmy, "mark my words."

But after a year, Bertie's dad got to like Jimmy and never said anything again about him. Indeed, when Jimmy used to slip him a £20 note, he would say, "He'll be a fine man one day, you wait and see." He usually said that on Saturday nights, half-pissed in the pub.

Bertie was like his dad, very broad, and was getting taller everyday. Not much to look at, but he had that lovely Irish sense of humour.

He could also fight. His dad made sure of that, taking him down the gym most Tuesday nights, with Bertie's uncle who used to box back in the old country. His uncle Sean used to say to his brother, "He'll be a tough bastard when he gets older." His dad would reply, "He's a tough bastard now."

School was out for Bertie. He gave it up when Jimmy was expelled for nicking the headmistress's handbag out of her study.

"Fuck em," Jimmy had said one day as he waited outside the school for Bertie and that was the day that Bertie left.

"I'm going to get a gang together," he had told Bertie one day. "And you're my number one, Bertie, OK?"

"You bet," Bertie had replied. "What we going to do, rob banks?"

Jimmy looked at him, his blue eyes broody. "One day, Bertie, one day."

* * *

Bertie could hear his mum, Mary, hoovering downstairs. "God," he said, "I wish Mum would give it a bloody rest."

He got ready, putting his beloved Dr Marten's on carefully; they looked dead smart with his Levi's and sweatshirt. He looked in the mirror, assessing his reflection. "Cool, son, cool," he said to himself. He opened his bedroom door, walked out and into the bathroom, brushed his teeth, washed his face and hands (his hair was too short to comb), grinned at himself in the mirror, had a quick wee, opened the bathroom door and walked out.

As he walked into the kitchen, his mum called out to him from the living room: "Jimmy boy called this morning; said he had to go out, but will meet you at 11.30 at Mac's in the high street."

"Oh, thanks, Mum. Did he say what he was doing this morning?"

"No, son, he didn't," his mother replied and continued with her cleaning.

Bertie looked at his watch, it was just gone 11am.

"Time for a quick cup of tea and a bacon sandwich," he said to himself. "Mum, don't you want to do me a ...?"

"Yes, yes, give me a minute," she said, reading his thoughts.

He walked into Mac's just after 11.40am. Jimmy was near the window, just about to light a fag.

"Want one?" he said to Bertie as he approached him.

"Just put one out, Jimmy, thanks," he said, sitting down opposite him. "What's to do today, mate?" He looked at Jimmy, seeing a bit of a frown on his face. "You don't look all that happy, mate."

"Er, it's nothing, Bertie. Been talking to old Mrs Lyons, you know, the old lady who lives near me, you know, her old man's a cripple."

"Yeah, yeah. Why, what's wrong, Jimmy? Ain't died has she or something? She's a nice old lady, the old man is a nice bloke as well."

Jimmy looked at his mate. "A bunch of Asian kids mugged her husband last night, broke his leg and fractured his bloody arm as well. They took all his money, even took his fags, the bastards. He's seriously ill in hospital. Not expected to live!"

"Bloody hell," Bertie blurted out. "We gonna do anything about it?" He stood up, looked around the restaurant. He punched his fist into his own hand. "I wish there were some in here, I'll fucking show em!"

"Sit down, sit down," Jimmy said to him. "I've already got it sorted, sit down, Bertie, and listen."

"Sorry, Jimmy, go on, go on. I'm listening."

"Well," Jimmy went on, "I've been out since 7 this morning, asking about what happened last night. Anyway, the story goes that the old man was coming back from the social club on the estate, about 10.30, but on the way to the lift to his flat, he realised that he'd left his glasses in the club. Anyway, as you know, Bertie, old man Lyons can't walk very fast, so by the time he got back to the club, it was closed.

"I can guess the rest, Jimmy," Bertie interrupted, "Them bastards must have seen him, and done him over."

"Yeah, Bertie, that's what happened. But unknown to them – there were six of them, by the way – up on the second floor of the flat, Dean Conte, the Italian kid, was having a crafty smoke. If his dad caught him smoking he'd bleeding kill him, that's why he was out there. Anyway, he told me this morning that about 11 he heard a lot of shouting, walked to the end of his balcony, looked over and saw the Pakis giving old man Lyons a kicking. He couldn't help so he ran back to his flat and told his dad, who phoned the Old Bill."

"What happened then?" Bertie said to Jimmy. "Did they arrest them?"

"Are you kidding, Bertie?" Jimmy looked at him. "They get away with murder, mate. Dean wouldn't tell them anything. No witnesses, no crime. They took all six of them down the nick, but let them go early this morning. Know what I mean?"

"Yeah," Bertie replied, "fucking bastards, they ain't getting away with that. . . ain't that right, Jimmy?"

"You have got it, mate. Anyway, I've found out from Dean that one of the Paki boys lives over near Kings Cross. Him and his mates go to a school over there."

"What we going to do, mate?" Bertie looked at him eagerly. "Are we having some of it?"

"You betcha life, Bertie. Old Mrs Lyons does our washing and things for us, I owe her and her husband big time. This is what you do – go round the boys up, I want them over Kings Cross by 3, outside the Drummond Street end of it. Also, get some of the boys from the old school. I'll round up about ten to fifteen myself. That should bring a nice number, about 40. Get 'em tooled up – baseball bats, knives, anything that hurts. When you get to Drummond Street, spread out, hide in doorways, don't act daft. I'll watch the school with Dean. He'll show me who the Pakis are, they all look alike to me. I'll follow them down the street from behind, so they can't run back. Hit 'em hard, Bertie, and then get the hell out of there before the Old Bill come. Do damage, don't hold back, I want these bastards hurting, OK?"

"All the way, Jimmy, all the way," Bertie smiled at him. "You gonna get the main one then?"

"Of course I am, what do you think?" Jimmy replied. He looked at his watch. It was just 2pm. "Blimey, I didn't think it was that late. You get over the estate and school, Bertie. I'll round up the rest of the boys. I'll see you at the bundle. Don't forget to get the tools. I'll see you there."

They both got up and walked into the high street.

Jimmy looked at Bertie. "Later..." he said, and walked away, leaving Bertie to get organised.

* * *

The revenge attack went down well. Owing to the surprise that Jimmy's gang sprung, the Asian kids stood no chance. Out of the 80 or 90 kids fighting, ten were stabbed, twelve were battered around the head but weren't too hurt, with cuts and bruises all around. One Asian girl who thought she could fight had her nose and arm broken.

Jimmy and Dave (Mack the Knife) cornered the Asian gang leader, with the help of some of Jimmy's gang and carried him over to a derelict building.

"Right, hold him down," Jimmy told some of his gang. "Bertie, hold his arm out over that lump of wood there."

Bertie held his arm out by sitting on it. "What you going to do, Jimmy?"

"Hold 'im mate," Jimmy said. He looked around, saw no one coming, put his hand into his overcoat and took out an old axe. He looked down at the young Asian who was shaking and crying with fright. "That is for the old man you gave a kicking to last night." He lifted the axe above his head and brought it down in one swift arc. The Asian kid's hand came clean away from his wrist as the axe made a clean cut through the bone. The boy fainted.

Jimmy stooped down, no emotion in his face at all, then picked the bloody hand up and started laughing. He walked over to the corner of the building, took a small can out of his pocket, dropped the hand onto the ground, sprayed it with the fluid from the can, took a box of matches from his pocket, lit one and set fire to the hand.

He looked around at his mates who were still shocked by this grotesque violence.

"Fucking hell, Jimmy," Dave said to him.

"Shut it Dave, he had it coming."

"Bleeding right!" the other boys shouted across to him.

"Nice one, Jimmy, that will teach 'em a lesson," Bertie said, a smile on his face.

"Fucking right, it will," Micky the Ferret said, now over the shock. "If they want more, they can have it," he went on.

"Yeah, yeah, come on fellas. We better push off quick, the Old Bill will be here soon, and we don't want to be around."

Jimmy looked around at his small gang. He knew they

33

wouldn't say anything to anyone, no matter what. He felt good and safe. No one else had seen what he had done, so he knew his secret was safe with this lot.

He walked over to the Asian who was still out. Jimmy kicked him in the balls, took out his penis and pissed all over him.

Chapter 4

BILLY DAY PUT DOWN THE LOCAL PAPER HE HAD BEEN READING AND GLANCED ACROSS AT HIS SON JIMMY.

"I suppose you were involved in the big fight down the Cross Monday then, you and your cronies. Looks like a lot of damage done. One poor kid lost his hand." He looked at Jimmy again. "Who would do a thing like that I wonder?"

Jimmy stood up and looked across at his dad. He said quietly, "My fucking heart's bleeding for 'em. That poor kid, as you say, did over an old bloke in his eighties. Six of them kicked the fuck out of him." Jimmy glared at his dad. "And did you know that the old bloke, Mr Lyons is now in hospital fighting for his fucking life? So don't you bleeding tell me, you bastard, what's wrong and what's right. You don't have any idea what goes on out there on them bloody streets day or night," Jimmy said to him now fuming.

He turned his back on his dad and walked over to the window. He looked up and saw the sun breaking through the clouds again. It was still quite warm. He looked at his watch, it was just after 6pm. He looked down at his young brother Mark who was writing something in his school book.

"I'll never get you involved in my business, bruv, I promise you that," he said to himself. "Hey Mark, fancy a movie tonight? Come on, I'll treat you, fish and chips after, what do you say?"

"Cor!" Mark looked up at him, then across to his dad. "Can I go Dad, please?"

"Yeah, course you can. Have a good time." He looked across at Jimmy as if to say something, but changed his mind.

Jimmy, no matter how much he hated his dad, never ever said anything about it to his young brother. He would always keep it like that until he was ready to do otherwise.

"What's on, Jimmy, anything good then?"

His big brother looked down at him again and said "Don't know, bruv, gimme the local up here and I'll have a look."

Mark got up, put his school books away, walked over to his dad's chair and picked up the local paper. He looked at the front page as he handed it over to his brother.

"Blimey, see this Jimmy," he said pointing to the front page.

It read, "Gang war on streets of Kings Cross. Young Asian boy loses his hand in racist attack".

"I'm not interested," he said to Mark and turned the pages over until he came to the entertainment section.

"What is it, Thursday, ain't it? Let's see." His eyes travelled down the page until he spotted what he wanted.

"Here we are at Holloway, you've got Batman starring

George Clooney. That won't be much cop, he's a crappy actor ... and let's see. . ." his finger went lower down the page. He stopped "What about this then ... Kim Basinger in LA Confidential?"

"Yeah," his brother said, a cheeky grin on his face.

"Wouldn't mind giving her one, Jimmy, know what I mean?"

Jimmy laughed at his young brother. "Yeah, wouldn't we all" he said. "On the way down, I'll see if Bertie and Dave want to come with us, OK?"

"Yeah, OK, Jimmy, I'll go and get ready."

Jimmy watched his brother go into his bedroom, then looked across at his dad, who, as usual, had fallen asleep.

"On the piss again. One day, mate, one day ...," he murmered to himself, looking scornfully at his old man.

He walked past his dad, opened the doors to the small balcony and stepped out on to it.

Jimmy lent over the small railing and looked down at the ground 18 floors below.

He looked at his watch; it was just after 6.30pm. The movie didn't start until 7.30pm so he had time to nip round for his mates. Except for Paul, Micky and the others were going to see Arsenal play. Jimmy wasn't into football, there were better things to do.

"Ready, Jimmy." The voice startled him. He straightened up off the rails and walked back into the living room.

"OK, Mark, let's go."

He didn't even look at his dad as he and his brother walked out of the flat.

They were all sat in the back row of the cinema, feet dangling over the seats in front. Bert was stuffing his face with popcorn and every other thing he could get in there. Dave was fast asleep, snoring his head off. Jimmy kept giving him a dig.

"How can he fall asleep when Kim Basinger's half naked on the screen bloody beats me, Dave," he managed to say between mouthfuls of popcorn.

"He's bloody nuts," piped up Mark looking at his brother.

"Shush, listen to the bloody film," Jimmy said to them, "let him bloody sleep."

"Jimmy, Jimmy," a voice came out of the darkness away to Dave's left.

"Who the fuck's that?" Jimmy said, trying to see in the darkened cinema.

It's me, Jimmy, Morris, you know, Morris Wright from the flats."

"What do you want? Can't you see we're watching the bloody movie?"

"I know, I know, but it's very important, might be of some interest to you, know what I mean?"

By this time, Morris had worked his way up to the seat in front of Jimmy.

"Can't it bloody wait, mate? Every time I get into this film, someone interrupts."

"Sorry, Jimmy," Morris said.

"That's all right. Now what's so important to stop me watching Kim getting screwed, it'd better be bloody good."

"Well, you know my old man works down the Caledonian Road in that warehouse?"

"Yeah, yeah, get on with it," Jimmy said, looking daggers at him. "So what's fucking urgent about that."

Morris went on, "Well, the other night he was talking to his mate who works with him and I heard my old man's mate tell him about the money they leave in there on Friday nights.

"Oh yeah?" Jimmy said. "I can see them leaving bloody money in there over the weekend, in a bloody meathouse, yeah, pull the other one."

"No, no, you don't understand," Morris said. "The reason the money's in there, Jimmy, is because the owner is a bloody Greek and he's on the fiddle ain't, he?"

Jimmy looked at Morris. "What you mean, on the fiddle? What's being a Greek got to do with it?" Jimmy looked at him waiting for an answer. "Well?"

"Most of the Greeks and Cypriots own fish and chip shops or food stores," Morris said, "even though they're the worst fish and chip fryers in the world."

"Bloody get on with it, Morris," Jimmy said, losing his patience.

"Sorry, Jimmy. Anyway, most of the money they take they ship back to the old country, don't they? You know, no money, no tax, know what I mean, Jimmy?"

"So you're saying that these Greeks, to avoid tax or whatever, take money out of the country illegally ... is that what you're telling me?"

"Yeah, that's it," Morris beamed at him.

"On a Friday night, some of them take their money over to my dad's place of work, and the owner, Stavros, ships it out for them. He doesn't know Dad knows anything about the money by the way."

"When does the money go then?" Bertie said leaning over the seat, "and why are you telling us," Jimmy said, reading Bertie's thoughts.

"I thought you might be interested," Morris said.

"And what's in it for you … and how much money are we talking about in the warehouse?" Jimmy asked.

"Just a nice earner for me, say about £500 – and to answer your next question, I should think about £20,000 in there."

"Fucking hell," Bertie said, "big time, we're not in to that much yet, are we, Jimmy?"

Jimmy looked at Bertie. "There's always a first time, mate."

"OK, Morris, I want to know everything about that bloody warehouse – how to get in, who's on guard, where the money's stashed, etc, etc. You with me?"

"Yeah, Jimmy, I've got it all for you. Here. . ." He reached inside the pocket of his coat and took out a folded sheet of paper. "It's all down there, everything you want to know."

"I'll look at this tonight when I get home. I'll let you know during the week. They do this run every week I hope." Jimmy said.

"No, it's done every fortnight on a Saturday morning very early."

Jimmy looked at him. "And it's due this week then," he said.

"No, next week, it will give you time to plan it, if you want to do it."

Jimmy leaned back and looked down the row at his young brother. He was too interested in the film to hear what they were saying.

"OK, Morris, we'll think about it. Come up to my flat Monday night. Me and the boys will have a meet, see what the score is. All right?"

Morris got up and shook hands with Jimmy and Bert. "See you Monday then, about 9. I'll ring you first." He got up and walked out of the cinema.

Bertie turned to Jimmy when he had gone and said, "Bit out of our league, mate, don't you think?"

"Maybe not, maybe not …" he replied. "We'll see, mate, let me think on it. Now enjoy the rest of the film."

Chapter 5

IT WAS MONDAY NIGHT. THEY ALL SAT THERE, ALL THE BOYS DRAPED IN THEIR ATTIRE. MORRIS LOOKED AT THEM, HE WANTED TO LAUGH, BUT HE KNEW IF HE DID THEY'D BREAK HIS LEGS.

"How did you get rid of your dad, Jimmy?" Micky asked him, "And where's Mark?"

"I got him to take my brother to a show up West, it cost me 50 quid." He looked across at Morris. "It had better be fucking worth it."

"Don't worry, Jimmy, it's going to be a doddle." Morris looked at him with a big smile on his face.

"Yeah, OK then," Jimmy said to them. All faces were turned to him, waiting for him to speak. Jimmy continued, "This is how it goes down. I've already been down to the warehouse over the weekend. I've clocked it. It looks so-so; I didn't find any cameras inside."

Micky interrupted. "Hang on, you mean you went inside … how'd you manage that then?"

"Easy, Micky, I went pretending I was looking for a job. Morris's dad don't work weekends so nobody knew me, right?"

"Yeah, very crafty, nice one, Jimmy," Dave said.

"So I went in and, just like Morris said, not very good security, but I did notice one camera on the outside, and, now I think about it, they can't really have a camera inside as it might pick up their little scam … see what I mean?"

"Great work," Paul White said, looking at Jimmy with admiration, "so we can go in Friday night then?"

"Not yet, mate, I've still got to look for a way in; it might be alarmed but I wouldn't think so, as they really wouldn't employ security in my opinion anyway."

He looked at Morris and said to him, "Can you find out from your dad about that mate, you know, a question here, a question there, find out all you can? I've got to know by Wednesday."

"You've got it, Jimmy." Morris looked at his watch, it was just after 10.30pm.

"I've got to go, Jimmy. I'll get all that for you if I can for Wednesday." He got up, nodded to the rest of the gang and walked out of the flat.

"You trust him, Jimmy?" Bertie asked his mate when Morris had gone.

"Yeah, I think so; anyway, he gave me that plan last Thursday about the layout for the job. He'll drop himself right in it if he talks. It was his idea anyway and I've got you to prove it, know what I mean?"

Sammy Jones spoke. He had a bit of a stutter and spoke very slowly "w – wh – where's the mo – m – money kept, Jim – Jimmy … has he – he told you y – yet?"

"Yes, he has, Sammy. You ain't going to believe this, boys, they keep it in a carcass of meat in the big freezer waiting to be picked up Saturday morning by one of the containers going to Greece. Quite clever, eh?"

He looked around them as they looked bemused.

"Bloody hell," Pete 'Looney Tunes' said, laughing, "very clever, very clever."

"OK, you lot, let's have ya. My old man will be back soon and I don't want him or Mark wondering why you are all here this time of night."

When they had gone, Jimmy went out to the balcony and lit up a fag. He looked down on the yard below, saw his gang coming out of the main door and shouted down for a laugh, "Keep the bloody noise down, you bloody hooligans."

He saw Bertie and Dave look up, knowing that it was him. They stuck their fingers up in the air at him and he could just about hear, "Fuck you."

He threw the butt down, put his arms above his head and yawned. Jimmy walked back in and sat down in his dad's chair. He reached across and picked up the phone (which he had had reconnected) and dialled Bertie's number. He waited a while and was just about to put the receiver down when it was picked up.

"Hello, who's that?"

"Oh hello, Mr Cooney, is Bertie in yet?"

He heard him shout to his son, "Bertie, Bertie, Jimmy on the phone." It went silent.

"Jimmy, what's up, mate?" Bertie asked.

"Nothing really, Bertie, just thought I'd tell ya, I don't trust Morris."

"Me neither mate. Anything you want me to do about it?"

"Yeah, get hold of Dave, tell him to follow him until we do the job, OK."

"Yeah sure, Jimmy, is that it? If so, I'm off to bed and see you tomorrow."

"Yeah, that's it Bertie, I'll see you down at Pancras Way at 12.00 tomorrow. Clear up that little thing I told you about. Oh, and by the way, tell the boys to come fully loaded tomorrow. See you, Bert."

Jimmy put the phone down, stood up and walked into his bedroom. As he started to get undressed, he heard his dad and brother come in. He walked out clad only in his boxer shorts.

"How'd it go, Mark?" he asked, looking across at his brother.

"Smashing, Jimmy, it was great, even Dad was dancing in the aisle."

Jimmy looked at his dad, who had sat down in his armchair by then.

"It's a bleeding change for him even to move." Jimmy looked back at his brother. "Right, I'm off to bed, see you in the morning. "Night, Mark."

He looked again at his dad and said, "Don't forget to lock up, there's a load of bleeding thieves around here."

Chapter 6

JIMMY WOKE UP JUST AFTER 10.30AM. HE GOT UP AND WASHED QUICKLY, GOT DRESSED AND WALKED OUT OF THE BEDROOM INTO THE KITCHEN.

His dad, as usual, was sat at the table, cigarette stuck in his mouth, reading the paper.

"Wanna cup of tea?" his dad asked, looking at him. He waited for a reply.

Jimmy looked at him, thinking to himself "he's after something."

"Yeah, please. Did Mark get off to school all right?"

"Yeah, I walked down with him, needed some sugar anyway, so nipped into the shop on the way back."

His dad got up, poured his son a cup of tea, looked over to him and said, "Want toast or something?"

"No thanks." He never called him 'Dad' and vowed he never

would. He sat down at the table as his cup was put in front of him. He looked up at him and said, "Ta."

"You out, today Jimmy?" his dad asked him.

"All day, so you'll have to get Mark's dinner for him. I'll leave you some money, save you cooking, not that you can bloody cook anyway."

"I can cook if I want to," Billy Day said, looking at his son.

"Yeah, when you're sober, so make do with a take-away. Mark likes Chinese, so get him that."

Jimmy looked at his watch, it was just after 11.30am, he'd have to go soon.

He walked back into the bedroom, knelt down at the side of the bed and reached under. He pulled out his cut-down baseball bat. He stood up, went to the wardrobe, and picked out his long coat. Before he put it on, he rolled the elastic band which kept the bat concealed up on his arm and secured it. He put his coat on, picked up his baseball cap and put it on.

He looked in the full-length mirror, liked what he saw and walked back into the kitchen. His dad had his back to him, washing his cup.

Jimmy put his hand into his jeans, took out a wad of money, unrolled £30 and put it on the table. He walked out of the kitchen and over to the front door. As he opened it, he shouted out to his dad, "The money's on the table for your teas. Keep the change." Knowing that he would, he walked out and slammed the door.

Jimmy walked slowly down the Pancras Way, behind King's Cross, thinking about why he was going there in the first place. His mind went back to last week when he had bumped into one of his many girlfriends' mothers, Mrs James.

"Jimmy, Jimmy, over here" she had shouted to him as he was walking down Kentish Town Road.

"Oh God," he had thought "I bet that bloody daughter of her's is up the spout. She told me she was on the pill'.

Jimmy pretended he hadn't heard her and made a bee-line for the post office. He went in and stood in the corner hoping that, if she came in, she wouldn't see him. She did and came over to him. "Jimmy, am I glad to see you … I need to talk to you."

"Mrs James, I can explain, if it's me I'll do good by her" he looked at her smiling.

She looked at him a bit bewildered. "What you on about, Jimmy. It's not Linda." She looked at him and burst out laughing.

"No, she ain't pregnant, it's about Mick, her brother."

"Wow, that's a relief Mrs James, I mean, we never really done anything, you know what I mean?"

"Yeah, pull the other one, Jimmy. Come over to the red cafe, have a cuppa with me. I need a word with you."

They sat down. Stirring her tea, Mrs James looked at him and said, "Someone down at Mick's school has been trying to sell crack to the kids."

"What?" Jimmy was really startled. "At Mick's school, you're having me on."

"No I'm not, Jimmy, a white bloke and a black geezer, they're about 25 years old. I've seen them a few times but thought they were picking up their kids, you know, you don't think about things like that happening. They're only five to fifteen year olds, kids, for God's sake – what scumbags would do that?"

"Are you sure, Mrs James, I mean 100 percent sure?"

"Call me Janet. Yes I'm bloody sure." She took out her fags. "Want one, luv?"

"No thanks, Mrs ... er ... Janet."

Jimmy looked at her. "Look Janet, I'll look into this OK? Leave it to me."

She looked at him, a big smile on her face and said, "I knew you would Jim, I ... "

"Jimmy, please, Janet, I hate the name Jim."

"Sorry. As I was saying, I know you hate drugs and you have a young brother yourself and our Linda said you were a bit of a hard-nut, even though you're only young. My old man's a bloody wimp. We need a few young ones about." A twinkle came into her eye. "Know what I mean, luv?" She laughed.

Jimmy got up, looked down at her and said smiling, "I'll see what I can do. On a Tuesday they're there, you said?"

"Thanks Jimmy, yeah Tuesdays. You're always welcome at our house you know."

As Jimmy walked back into the road, he thought to himself, "Yeah welcome in your house, but not to see Linda, I bet," he smiled.

Jimmy thought about the future. He had walked all this way thinking about what Janet James had told him. As he came into Pancras Way, he saw the rest of the boys sat around, but not all together.

"Good thinking," he thought to himself. Bertie must have split them up.

As Bertie came into view, Jimmy saw that he was sat on a low wall talking to Dave Smith and Paul White. They saw him coming and, as usual, Bertie got up and made his way towards him.

"Watcha, mate," he looked over his shoulder, "all here, Jimmy except Pete, he couldn't make it, had to go out with his dad to fetch a cooker they'd bought on the cheap."

That's OK, don't think we'll need him." He glanced at his watch – 12.15pm.

"Right, the kids come out for lunch about 12.50, right?" He looked at his mate.

"Yeah, right mate. I asked my mum's friend Mrs Brady, she's a dinner lady here. She said the kids usually run out into the yard about 12.55" Bertie said, looking at his friend. "Why?"

"Well, Janet James reckons them geezers come round about 1 and talk to the kids through the railings, but today they're in for a bit of a surprise, ain't they?"

"They bloody well are, old son."

"Less of the old, Bertie. Come on, let's get the boys together. I've got a nice little plan."

They were all sat around on the wall, waiting for Jimmy to talk to them.

"Dave, did you get hold of Lenny Mason?"

"Yep, Jimmy, he should be here soon."

"OK, now listen up. I've asked Lenny to come and give us a hand; he's a bit of a villain and will do anything for money. This is what we're going to do."

"Janet says them geezers stand over the back of the school near those railings. See 'em over there?" he said, pointing over to the school. "They stand there 'cos the school teachers or caretaker can't see them, it's on an angle, you see. Anyway, when we see them we are gonna rush them, suprise and all that. Bundle them in the back of the van and go from there."

"Yeah, it's going to be that easy, ain't it" Micky the Ferret, said to Jimmy laughing.

"It will be, believe me. Have you seen the size of Lenny? He stands 6ft 3in, weighs about 20st. He'll get them, you wait and see."

As he finished talking, a white transit van pulled up across the road.

"Hi, Jimmy," a voice boomed across the road.

"Shush, keep your voice down, Lenny. Do you want the whole world hanging around here?"

Jimmy walked across the road to the van. He waited until Lenny got out. Long hair, scruffy beard and boy, was he big.

"Hello, mate," Jimmy said to him, "dead on time. Come on, I'll introduce you to the rest of the boys."

"Hang on, hang on, Jimmy, money up front, remember."

"Oh, sorry, Lenny." Jimmy dipped into his back pocket, bringing out a white envelope. "Here, 500 wasn't it? Did you bring the tape and rope?"

"Yeah, everything's in there, Jimmy, don't worry. Where are them bastards? Anything to do with kids makes my bloody blood boil."

"Jimmy, Jimmy, they're here," Dave said as he ran across to him and Lenny. "They're doing exactly as Janet James said they would."

"Right, Lenny, get the van as near to them as you can. Me and the boys will just pretend we're going by and we'll make the switch, but, Lenny, I want you with me, Dave and Bertie, OK?"

"OK, Jimmy, leave it to me."

Lenny got in the van and drove it around to the school which was on the corner.

"Come on, boys, half with me. Dave, Bertie, Sammy, you lot get over the other side of the road. Only come over if we need you. Micky, you keep watch, let us know when the road is clear, OK?"

They split up; Jimmy and his half going off first, Micky and the rest following on the other side.

As Jimmy rounded the corner of the school, he said to his mates "Dave, get your knife, stick it under the black man's throat. Bertie, get your club out, me and you will go for their legs, right?"

"With you, Jimmy," they both said together.

The two men were leaning on the fence, their backs to Jimmy's gang, oblivious to what was going on.

Lenny's van was parked 2ft away, the back doors open. Lenny was stood on the pavement pretending he was waiting for someone. As they came abreast of Lenny, Jimmy shouted, "Now, get on with it."

Dave's knife came out so fast, he said later it was quicker than a gun draw. He put the knife under the geezer's chin and said, "Move it you arsehole, in the van ... one false move and you're dead."

Bertie and Jimmy had the other guy off the pavement before he knew what was happening and they were both thrown in the back of the van. Lenny jumped in after them. They had their arms tied and mouths gagged before they knew what had hit them. They didn't have time to struggle.

The rest of the gang jumped in the back.

"OK, Lenny, let's go to the lock-up."

Lenny got up, jumped out of the van and walked to the front, climbed in, started up the motor and drove up and down

Pancras Way, around Royal College Street, backwards and forwards for about half-an-hour to fool them.

Jimmy shouted to him from the back "OK, mate, in we go."

Lenny went down the side of St Pancras Station. All along Midland Road there were lock-up garages. Jimmy had already rented one over the phone a week earlier, and the key was sent to a different address. It was just the job.

Lenny got out, unlocked the sliding door, opened it, jumped back in behind the wheel and drove inside. He got out again, pulled the main door down and banged on the back of the van.

"Out you come, boys," he said.

When they were out, Jimmy looked at them. "OK, boys," let's see what our packages have to say."

They pulled the two men out and dumped them on an old mattress on the floor. Jimmy ripped the tape off their mouths. He sat down in an old chair opposite them.

"Now, lads, what's this I hear about you two trying to sell drugs to our kids? Got something to tell us?"

The black one spat on the side of the mattress. He spluttered, eyes blazing.

"What the fuck do you think you're doing whitey?" he glared at Jimmy "a bunch of fucking kids, what's fucking going on?"

Jimmy stood up, took his club out from his coat, walked over to the man and smacked him right across the cheek with it. Blood spurted out, followed by a few teeth.

"You bastard, you're fucking dead, you motherfucker."

Jimmy hit him again, this time across the legs, but not too hard.

"Are you going to answer the question or not?" Jimmy said to him.

"No chance, you prick," he spat his blood and saliva all over Jimmy's boots and coat.

Jimmy stepped back, looked down at his boots, and saw the blood dripping off his coat. He looked up again and turned to Dave.

"Put his gag back on …"

Jimmy put his hand in his pocket and took out a pair of leather gloves. He slowly put them on, cracking his knuckles as he did so.

When Dave had put the tape gag back on the black guy, Jimmy turned to Micky the Ferret and said "Gimme your club, it's longer than mine."

"Sure, Jimmy." Micky passed it over and stood back. So did the others. They knew what was coming, they'd seen it before.

Jimmy put the baseball bat above his head, looked down at the black guy and said, "Nobody calls me 'whitey' you fucking scumbag," and brought the club down so hard on the black man's legs it brought tears to Micky's eyes.

A muffled groan came from the drug-dealer as Jimmy brought the club down again and again until he couldn't lift the club anymore.

As cool as ever, he gave the club back to Micky and said to him smiling, "Burn that down the tip, I'll get another one."

He bent down and pulled the white man's tape off. As he did, terror came into the man's eyes.

Jimmy said to him, "What's your name, mate?" as if nothing had happened.

"John Bates … please, let me go."

"I'm going to, Johnny," he said as he patted his cheek. "You get the message ... don't ever fucking sell drugs to kids again. I'll find out and I'll fucking kill you."

"I won't, I won't." The man was shaking. "Please don't hurt me."

Jimmy looked across at Lenny. "Take him out, mate." He looked down at the man again.

"Where you live, Johnny boy?"

"Birmingham, we come down twice a week and ..."

Jimmy cut him short. "Don't fucking come down again. You thicko's stay in your own rubbish tip, got it."

"Yes, mate ... yes mate ... don't worry, I will."

"Empty your pockets." Jimmy said to him. Looking at Dave, he said, "Cut them ropes off him."

Dave cut the ropes and helped the man up.

When he had emptied his pockets, Jimmy counted £300 in notes and two bags of crack, which he stamped on.

"Here," he gave the man back £40. "Your lucky day. Now fuck off and don't come back. And if I see you back in London ..."

"OK, you lot in the van. Take this bag of shit back to Euston, make sure he gets on the train."

He gave the money he had left to Dave to share out with the boys.

"Bertie, you stay with me. The rest of you, I'll see you Thursday over at the pub."

When they had all gone, Bertie turned to Jimmy and pointed to the black guy lying unconscious. "What about him Jimmy?"

"Watch and learn, Bertie."

He picked up an old iron pole lying on the floor, walked over to the man on the mattress, looked down at him and smiled. He then smashed the pole down on the man's head until Bertie pulled him off.

"For fuck's sake, Jimmy, that's enough, let's fuck off."

Jimmy laughed, threw the pole down and picked up the crushed drugs. He sprinkled it all over the now dead man and said laughing wildly, "Ashes to ashes. You won't be selling drugs to kids again, mate. Come on, Bertie, let's go."

"What about his pockets, Jimmy, you gonna go through 'em? Might have a lot of dough on him."

"Na, leave it, the cops will think it's a gangland killing," Jimmy replied. "And wrap that pole up. We'll take it with us. I'll get rid of it down Tony Murphy's scrapyard later tonight."

Chapter 7

DAVE 'MACK THE KNIFE' SMITH WAS JUST ABOUT TO FINISH HIS DINNER WHEN HIS MUM ROSE CAME INTO THE KITCHEN. HE HAD THE FORK TO HIS MOUTH. SHE LOOKED AT HIM, SEEKING OUT HIS EYES.

In her hand she had the local paper. She threw it across the table at him. "I hope you're not involved with this David." She always called him David; he hated it.

He put the last forkful into his mouth, chewed, swallowed, belched, then looked up at his mum. "Involved in what, Mum?" He looked at her, innocence written all over his face.

"Look at the bloody paper. This looks like local work to me and it reads between the lines 'Jimmy Bloody Day', the young thug, your mate."

Dave picked up the paper. He never read the local which came through the letter box every Thursday. He glanced at the front page, stood up and walked over to the window for a better light to read it. He also knew more or less what it contained, and he didn't want to let his mum see the reaction on his face, if any.

He murmured to himself as he read the article: GANGLAND KILLING IN KINGS CROSS ARCHES. That was the headline. He looked down the page and read on:

> *Leroy Deacon, a black Jamaican, was found Tuesday morning in a lock-up garage in King's Cross. He had been bludgeoned to death. Mr Deacon's legs were also broken. Crack cocaine was found spread all over his body. In his pockets, police found £600 in notes and also several packets of crack.*
>
> *Chief Inspector Davies of King's Cross Police said to the Journal, "I and my colleagues believe that Mr Deacon was involved in a gangland killing. There are a lot of drugs in King's Cross."*
>
> *"Are you closer to catching the killer or killers, Inspector?" Ian Dome, our reporter, asked him.*
>
> *"Not at this precise time, but we will catch them, believe me."*

Dave threw down the paper on the table and laughed. He looked at his mum keeping his face as straight as he could and said, "Way out of Jimmy's league, Mum, he wouldn't get into that, believe me."

"Not what I've bloody heard. He's an evil bastard that one, the talk's all round the estate."

"Rubbish, Mum."

"Who's evil then?" A voice issued from the doorway of the kitchen.

"Jimmy Day, Dad, that's what Mum reckons."

"Bollocks, Jimmy's all right," Peter Smith said, sitting down at the kitchen table and reaching for the paper.

He read a bit of the front page, looked up at his wife and son and said, "Murder, you've got to be kidding, he's only ..."

"I know, I know, a kid," Rose interrupted. "So was bloody Mary Bell, she was only fucking 11. I bet Jimmy's involved in this somewhere along the line, you can bet your bloody life on that." With that, she walked out of the kitchen slamming the door behind her.

"Wow, what's got into her this morning?" Dave's dad said to him through a mouthful of pasta.

Dave looked at his dad, shrugged his shoulders and said, "You know Mum, Dad, listening to all that gossip."

"Yeah, son, I know, I know."

"Right, got to go Dad, I'll see you later then."

"Yeah, see you, son," and he carried on reading the paper.

Pete Smith read a bit more of the story but soon got fed up reading about it, saying to himself, "How these people can get involved in drugs and things beats me."

He got up, picked up his empty cup and plate, walked over to the sink, dropped them in it and walked out of the kitchen door.

As he went to get his coat and hat, Rose came out of their bedroom where she had been hovering. She looked at her husband and said, "What do you think then Pete, is Dave's mate involved or what? If he is, I don't want him hanging around our son and that's a bloody fact, I can tell you."

Pete looked at his wife; they had been married for 20 or so years, and had only two children, Sue and Dave, both still at home. Sue worked down the bakers in the high street, she was 18.

Dave, well, he was 16 and had never worked but always had money. Pete hadn't worked for over ten years, having lost his job as a printer.

"Fuck 'em Rose. When the Government said they would change the face of Britain, they really meant it. It's all bleeding coloured faces here now, except a few white ones." Pete looked over to his wife and said, "Look, luv, Dave knocks around with who he likes, I can't stop him, you can't stop him and, as for Jimmy Day, he's OK, he helped us out last month when we owed all that rent money. The council were going to evict us if it weren't for him. I'll never forget that and, as far as I'm concerned, he's all right, so forget about it, OK."

Rose looked at Peter. Since he had lost his job, he'd got lazy and had slowly put on weight and always looked scruffy. She couldn't stand him anymore and only stayed because of the children. She didn't need him now. If he only knew that she was screwing his best mate and had been for the past two years. She wondered if he'd change, but doubted it.

"Well, I'm not going down on my knees and thanking God for bleeding Jimmy Day. He's a fucking evil little bastard, everyone knows it. What, are you thick or something?" She looked at him, her eyes blazing, "Do you want your son to end up in jail then, do you?"

Pete looked at her, opened the door and thought to himself, "Now's not the time for an argument," walked out and closed the door on her.

He walked down the stairs in the block of flats they lived in, hoping she wouldn't come after him. His wife had the foulest mouth on the whole estate, and it was nice to get away from her for a couple of hours.

Today, he was off up the billiard hall to have a few games with his mate. He stepped out into the courtyard on the northern side of the vast estate they lived on. Jimmy and the rest of Dave's mates lived in the east end of the estate.

"Hi, Peter," said a voice from behind.

A man about 6ft stood to the right of him – grey suit, hat, polished black shoes.

"Well, well, well, if it ain't Sergeant Ken Sanders, CID. You're taking a risk coming round here, Kenny boy, you might get mugged."

Sergeant Sanders looked at him with contempt. "You don't want to take the piss, Pete, we might meet up on a dark night." He looked at Peter with anger in his eyes. "Know what I mean, as you Londoner's say?" He continued, "Is your boy Dave in? If he is, I'd like a word with him."

"You wanna talk to my boy, copper?" Pete said angrily. "You got a fucking warrant?" He started to walk away.

"Hold on, hold on, I just wanna know where he was last week when that young Paki kid lost his hand in the gang fight … you must have read about it."

"No I didn't," Pete replied. "Don't read the paper much anyway; crap like that doesn't interest me," he said walking away.

The cop stood there looking at Peter Smith's retreating back. "You ignorant bastard, I'll have that fucking boy of yours and the rest of the gang, mark my words," Ken Sanders said to himself, kicking a brick away which was on the road in front of him and, in doing so, he hurt his big toe. "Bastard," he muttered to himself.

Ken Sanders had been a copper for 25 years, not far off retirement, and he wanted to go out in a blaze of glory. He had come down from Glasgow 15 years earlier, first to Stratford then to Camden which he liked. The crime rate had gone down for a while in the Eighties but, thanks to drugs, had increased a hundred-fold in the Nineties.

He knew most of the villains but it was the young guns who scared him. They didn't know fear. Young kids aged between ten and seventeen were doing most of the crime and getting away with it.

"You're going to stop it aren't you, Sergeant?" his Chief had said to him "Or you won't see another promotion. Get out there. Pick your own men and get on with it. I'll give you a year to clear the bloody mess up." And here he was trying his damndest and it was bloody hard work.

He knew a young gang was operating around North London. He knew all their names and where they lived. He even knew when most of them went for a crap, but he couldn't get to hear one word said against them. A copper's nightmare. "The code of honour," he thought to himself. "What would happen if every fucker in the world went on the code; you wouldn't need fucking coppers."

He kicked the brick again, forgetting he'd already kicked it before, and jumped at the pain in his toe.

"Shit, shit." He was really angry now and hoped that he'd bump into some villians but he didn't. He walked back to the police car which was unmarked, opened the passenger door and climbed in.

"How'd you get on Serge?" asked Detective John Rowly, his partner, who was sitting in the driving seat. Ken Sanders looked at him. "Bloody awful … I bumped into his dad, who wasn't too pleased to see me. Told me to get an effing warrant, which I can't as we don't have any bloody proof or witnesses. I'll get something on him, somehow, then I'll bring him in." He looked at his partner. "Back to the station, John. Let's look at those statements again; might find something on that gang. Let's go."

Chapter 8

BERTIE COONEY WAS SAT CROSSED LEGGED ON DAVE SMITH'S LIVING ROOM FLOOR. DAVE HAD TOLD JIMMY THAT HIS MUM AND DAD WOULD BE OUT FOR THE EVENING. MUM AT BINGO, HIS DAD AT THE LOCAL PUB, SO THEY COULD COME AROUND TO HIS PLACE TO PLAN THE ROBBERY AT THE WAREHOUSE.

"So what was so important you wanted to tell me, Dave?" Jimmy asked him while he struggled to open a can of beer.

Dave looked at him, laughing. "Want me to open that beer for you, mate? You're struggling there."

"Get on with it, Dave, what d'you hear?"

"Well, Jimmy, Dad said that a local copper was asking about me, said he wanted to talk to me about that Asian fight last week."

"And?" Jimmy said looking at him suspiciously.

"Nothing, Jimmy, my old man told him to fuck off and get a warrant, but he won't be back, believe me."

"OK, let's forget about it, right? Is everyone here?" Jimmy said looking around.

"Yeah, all here, Jimmy," Bertie said.

"Well, boys," Jimmy said, "I've been again to the warehouse and I can tell you I've found a way in; it's a bit dangerous but we can do it. I went up to the warehouse roof, me and Bertie," he looked across at his best mate, "who I may say nearly fell off the fucking roof and took me with him."

Bertie looked at him. "Yeah," he laughed, "bit of a laugh, though, wasn't it?"

"Anyway," Jimmy went on, "we got on top of the roof by climbing up the brick wall at the back of the warehouse. It was quite easy. As we reached the top of the wall there were a couple of old scaffolding tubes leading from the wall to the top of the warehouse roof. It looks like someone else has been up there quite a long time ago and left the poles behind or forgot them. Anyway, we got on the roof, looked around and found an old skylight open. The stench coming out of there was unbelievable. The skylight opened easily and there's one of them ladders going down to the first floor, so that's the way in tomorrow."

"So who's actually going, Jimmy?" Sammy Jones asked, "or are we all going in together?"

"Yeah, Jimmy, I want some of the action," Pete Higgins blurted out.

Bertie looked at Pete, laughing. "There's no way you're coming up on the roof with me, Looney. I want to come down in one piece."

The others laughed.

"Yeah," Jackie "Sweeney" Todd said, "I ain't going up on the bloody roof for love, or money, I can tell you."

"Shut up and listen will ya!" Jimmy said, looking at them, "me and Bertie will go up and do all the monkey work; you lot stay down and keep watch. I'm bringing big Lenny in on this."

"What the fuck for?" shouted Sammy "We don't need him, do we, Jimmy?"

"We might," Jimmy said, "he can stay down on the ground with Dave. You never know, might need a bit of help on the ground. Anyway, we are going to need his motor and, by the way, he doesn't know how much or why we're going in. He most probably thinks we're going to nick meat or whatever."

"How much you paying him, Jimmy?" Micky asked.

"If the money's there and we get away with it, I'll give Lenny 1,000. It'd fucking better be there or Morris is a dead 'un. Lenny did well on that drug thing."

"Anway, meet me and Bertie and Dave near the old gasworks, you know, round the back there, but don't all come together. I want you all there by 12pm, OK? No shirkers, so if you can't come, tell me now."

"I won't be able to come, Jimmy. Mum and Dad are taking me and my sister out for a meal, it's Mum's birthday. Sorry, mate," Paul White said to him.

"That's OK, Paul as long as you've told me and keep quiet about it – right?"

"'Course, Jimmy, who do you think I fucking am? I never say nothing to nobody."

"All right, all right, mate," Jimmy said, "have a good time anyway."

"Hang on, hang on … is he getting the same money as us then?" Micky spoke up looking at Jimmy.

"Yes he is, he's in the gang ain't he? You all would get the same if you were here or not." He looked around at the others. "Any more moans?"

Nobody spoke up, so Jimmy carried on, "Morris has told me where the money will be. They keep it in a plastic bag well taped up, and then they put it inside the carcass and sew it up again. It's very rare the Customs men look in these containers as they're mostly sealed. Anyway, the Customs men are most probably on the take; that's how they get the money through I should think. Me and Bertie will go down into the warehouse. Morris's dad or his mate won't be around. I'll go straight to the containers which aren't sealed until they get to the docks. Once I'm in, I'll take the money out, take it out of the bag, put a bit of meat in the bag instead, seal it up, tape it again and sew the carcass up again. Easy, he said, looking around at his gang, all looking at him in amazement.

"Wow, Jimmy, you're great," Dave Smith said, "some plan."

"Yeah, I know," Jimmy said. "Any questions?"

Micky put his hand up.

"Yeah, Micky, what's up?" Jimmy said to him.

"How do you know it's going to be in English money?" Micky asked, looking at him.

"Good question, Micky."

Micky looked around at the rest of the gang, waiting for praise; none came.

"Morris told me they always send it in English notes 'cause they get a better interest rate, OK. Any more questions?" Jimmy said.

"When are we going to share the money out, Jimmy, and how much do we all get?" Jackie Todd asked, a glint in his eye.

Jimmy looked around at all the gang and knew that they all trusted him completely.

"Right." he said. "Out of the 20,000, I'm giving 1,000 to Lenny, OK? I'm giving 1,000 to Mrs Lyons to see her by, you know, while her old man's in hospital … and the rest, well, the only way to do it fairly is like this. We'll have 18 grand left; I'm splitting it up so Bertie will get 3,500. I'll get 5,500 and the rest of you will get 1,500 each. Me and Bertie are getting more 'cause we're taking all the risks and also I'm getting more 'cause I planned it as well. Any questions?" He looked around at them, waiting.

Dave stood up. "That'll suit me fine, mate. You and Bertie are doing all the work, you deserve it and it's your gang anyway."

"Great, Jimmy. Cor, what am I going to do with all that dough?" Pete said.

"Let's hope we do it right, then let's celebrate," Micky said.

"He's right," Sammy Jones added, "it's nice but let's wait."

"You won't be able to spend the money for a while anyway until things cool down. You can't flash big money around like that at your age, know what I mean?" Bertie said to them all.

"He's right, we'll sort that out after the job. Is that it then, anything else?"

Nobody said anything. Jimmy looked at his watch, it was just after 10.30pm.

"Thanks, Dave, for letting us round; we'd better shoot off, your mum and dad will be home soon and we all know what your mum thinks of me. Come on you lot, let's nip over to the chippie, I'm bleeding starving and it closes at 11."

"Sorry I couldn't give you something to eat, Jimmy, you know my mum, she labels and marks everything."

"Don't worry, mate, it's nothing. Look, I'll see you in the morning or are you coming down to the fish shop with us?"

"No thanks, Jimmy, I've got to stay here, it's a bit late and my dad will do his nut if I go out this late. I'll see you all tomorrow night, OK, at 12.30."

Jimmy walked to the door with the rest of the gang behind him. He looked across at Dave saying, "I'll see you at 12.30 tomorrow night, Dave. Can't see you in the day as I've got to do a lot of planning. Me and Bertie have got to see someone about a bit of money owing to us. By the way, don't forget to collect that money off the gay guy, the Asians and that Italian geezer up at Highgate."

"Who should I take with me, Jimmy?" Dave asked him.

"Take Paul here and Micky. Bring the money back to your house and stash it. I'll split it up Saturday after the job – all right? Come on boys, let's get some supper, my treat."

* * *

"Who taught you to fry fish and chips, Eddie?" Jimmy asked the Greek fish shop owner.

"I taughta myself, why?" Eddie said, looking at Jimmy, knowing he was taking the piss.

"You can tell," Pete said to him. "This fish is still alive."

"Yeah, and my chips are so full of fat," said Jackie Todd, "they've been offered a part in Grease III, The Movie."

The rest of the gang all started laughing, but Eddie didn't take any notice as he got this most nights. "Come on boys, whatta you all having?" he asked, looking at them laughing. He didn't want to upset them as he knew they would wreck his shop if he did. "It's after 11."

After they had got their orders they all walked around to Hampstead Road and sat on the wall near the garage. It was open 24 hours a day, so if they wanted anything they usually went there.

Looney Tunes was throwing chips at the cars and buses going by. One of the other boys, Sammy, threw a big bit of fish which landed on the front of a taxi's windscreen. The cab driver pulled up 20 yards down the road, got out and wiped the fish off. He turned around to the gang and shouted back to them "You bleedin' hooligans, you could have made me crash!"

"Fuck off, you old git," shouted Paul.

"Yeah, piss off, you old Jew boy," Micky screamed at him.

They all stood up and started to walk towards the cab driver who by then was back in his cab and on his way, his hand stuck out of the window, fingers in the air.

"Wanker," shouted Bertie, "come back here, you bastard." But by then the cab had disappeared.

"Well, you lot, I'm going home; you coming Bertie?" Jimmy said looking at his mate. He checked his watch, it had just gone 12.

"Count me in, Jimmy." Bertie looked at the others. "What about you lot?"

Micky spoke up for the others. "Yeah, we're off as well, we'll see you all tomorrow. 'Night, Jimmy … see you, Bertie." They all said their goodbyes as they walked off in separate directions.

By the time Jimmy arrived home it was past 1am, he and Bertie had been talking for a while. He felt pretty tired as he unlocked his front door and walked in. He could hear his dad snoring. Jimmy walked through the passage way and looked in at his young brother. Mark was well gone, feet dangling out of the bed. It was very warm in there, so Jimmy opened his brother's window to let some fresh air in.

He walked back out and into the living room. Mark's case was laid on the floor half packed.

"Shit, I forgot Mark was going up to Alice's place for the summer holiday," Jimmy said out loud. "How could I bloody forget? Anyway, I'll see him in the morning before he goes" he murmured to himself.

Jimmy went to bed and slept like a log.

* * *

"Wake up Jimmy, wake up."

Jimmy felt himself being shaken. He opened his eyes. "What … who … what the fuck?"

"It's me, Jimmy, Mark … I'm off. Dad's taking me over to Euston. I'm catching that 9.30 to Manchester."

Mark looked at him, a tear in his eye. "My first time away from you and dad, Jimmy. I'm gonna miss you both."

"Hang on, bruv." Jimmy got out of bed and walked over to his jeans that were hanging over a chair. He put his hand into his back pocket and pulled out some money.

"Here," he counted off £100, "stick that in your bin. If you need any more, phone me … and tell Alice I'll try and get up there before you come back. Listen, I might even come up there with Bertie and fetch you back after your holiday – right?"

"Cor, that would be smashing, Jimmy." He gave his older brother a hug and walked out of the room saying "see you bruv."

Chapter 9

JIMMY AND BERTIE WERE WALKING DOWN TOTTENHAM COURT ROAD WHEN BERTIE PULLED HIM BY THE ARM. "LOOK WHOSE COMING TOWARDS US, JIMMY," HE SAID POINTING AHEAD OF THEM.

"Blimey, it's Linda James and her mates. Let's get across the road quick," Jimmy said to him.

"Too late, mate, they've already seen us."

"Shit, I didn't want to see her or anyone today of all days. If she stops, let's make it quick all right, Bertie?" he looked at his mate for support.

"Yeah, sure, Jimmy, I'll get rid of them, don't worry."

"Hello, Jimmy," Linda said as she came up to them, her mates trailing behind. "Mum said she was chatting to you the other day. You wanna watch her, she likes 'em young."

Jimmy laughed, "Yeah, I bet she does. Anyway, Linda, got to

go, ain't we, Bertie?"

Bertie nodded, "Yeah, we have and it can't wait."

"You going down the Palais tomorrow night, Jimmy?" Linda asked, waiting for an answer.

"Might be ... depends if I'm around. Me and the boys have been quite busy lately. I'll see."

She looked at him, "Can I say that's a date then, Jimmy?"

"Let's wait and see. I've got to go, honest. Look, I'll see you later. Come on, Bertie, let's go. Bye, girls."

They walked off to the sound of the girls giggling.

"She's really got the hots for you, mate," Bertie quipped.

"I've been with her and don't plan to go with her again, I can tell ya. I know what I'll do one night – I'll throw a party, get her and her mates round and let them gang bang her. She'll love that, she's sex mad. She wanted it night and day when I was knocking her off, greedy cow, and she's only 16. Come on, Bertie, let's go and see that bloke in the camera shop about a little extortion."

Bertie had turned the shop sign to "Closed" as they walked into the camera shop.

"Here, what you doing with that sign?" the owner said coming around the counter as he shouted at Bertie.

"Calm down, mate, calm down," Jimmy said to him from behind.

The man looked at him, then at Bertie. "Who the hell are you two and what you doing in my shop? If you want to buy, all well and good, if you don't, fuck off. Looking at you, I don't think you want to buy."

Jimmy looked at him and said with disgust, "I know all about you, you dirty little pervert, you're not interested in selling bloody cameras, you're into filming porn films. This is just a front this shop, ain't it, Alan?"

"How do you know my name, and you're talking rubbish. I've had this shop for years, it's been my hobby since I was ..."

Jimmy cut him off. "Yeah, yeah, who you trying to kid, Alan? I was told about you months ago. You're into everything mate – porn films, dirty books, photos, the lot. You dirty bastard, why don't you just admit it ... and I also know you make a lot of money out of it as well."

Bertie Cooney moved over to the now scared shopkeeper. Bertie looked at him and spat out, "It's a good job you're not into kiddy porn; you'd be dead by now, I can promise you that, you fucking piece of shit."

The shopkeeper looked at them both in turn. "How did you find out about me?" He asked, turning to Jimmy.

Jimmy looked at him. He was looking at a man about 5ft 6in tall, skinny, white-faced (more pasty-looking than white), about 60 years of age. He looked like a dirty old man. His clothes were loose on him, grotty, all he needed was a mac.

"We ain't going to hurt you, mate, don't worry. We just want to do a deal with you, that's all."

"Don't you mean blackmail me? Or is that above your intelligence?" the man said.

"Don't you get fucking funny, mister, don't let my looks fool you. I'd like to break your fucking legs and I could if I wanted, believe me. Now bleeding listen to me and listen good," Jimmy said. "You give me £500 here and now or I'm going to tell someone what you really do in here." He put his hand on the shopkeeper's shoulder. "You got that, Alan?"

"You wouldn't ... anyway, who'd believe two kids?" He looked at them feeling a bit braver.

"I'm more than a bloody kid, you runt. Don't fuck with me or you'll regret it, that I promise you," Jimmy snarled at him.

"All right, all right, I ain't got that sort of money in here. I'll get it for you on Monday, I promise."

"You better, mate," Bertie said, grabbing hold of the man's shirt and pulling his face up close to his, "you fucking better."

Jimmy looked at the shopkeeper, staring at him with evil in his eyes. "I'll send someone in for it Monday morning, and listen good – once a month I want £400, always on a Monday morning, and I want the money all in twenties, all right, you fucking low-life?"

"Yes, yes," the man was starting to blubber, "I'll get it for you, now please let me alone. Go, please."

Jimmy looked at Bertie smiling, "Come on, mate, let's piss off, this wimp's getting me down." Jimmy looked around him, walked behind the counter and helped himself to two Pentax cameras worth about £300. "You'll get these back when you pay up on Monday. Let's go," he nodded to Bertie.

They walked to the door, opened it and walked out into the street.

As they walked away from the shop, Bertie looked at Jimmy and said, "Think he'll come across, Jimmy?"

"He'll come across, don't worry about that," Jimmy looked at his mate. "Here," he said, throwing a camera to him, "give that to your dad."

"Cor, thanks, mate," Bertie said sticking the camera in his

coat pocket. "What you going to do with the other one?"

Jimmy smiled. "I'm gonna give it to my brother when he comes back, he'll like that."

* * *

Lenny was already there when Jimmy and Bertie arrived at the side of the warehouse. The three of them were hidden from view by an old tree whose roots had made the warehouse wall lopsided. Bertie looked at his watch then at Lenny and Jimmy, and he spoke quietly, looking right and left.

"It's just after 12 Jimmy, and nobody's here but us; what we going to do if nobody turns up?"

"Don't worry, mate, they'll turn up. Paul ain't coming anyway." Hearing a noise, Jimmy looked round. "There they come; told you not to worry."

Dave came up first, followed by Sammy, Micky, then Pete and Jackie.

"Whatcha, Jimmy, Bert. Hello, Lenny," they all more or less said at the same time.

"I thought I told you to spread out; are you bleeding daft coming here all at once?" Jimmy was fuming. He looked at Dave and said, "You should have known better, Dave."

"Sorry, mate," Dave said, going red in the face.

The others mumbled something which Jimmy couldn't make out.

"Right," he said, "hope you've emptied your pockets like I told you, don't want you dropping things, do we? Got your knife, Dave? If you have, keep it in your jeans, don't want you dropping that, mate, it's got your bloody initials on it."

"Didn't bring it, mate, didn't think I'd need it," Dave said to him.

"OK, you lot, now listen. Me and Bertie are going over the wall in a minute, so get in your places. Lenny, you stay here under the tree with Micky. Dave, you get over there on the other side of the road, take Sammy with you.

"Jackie, take Pete with you ... and no fucking about, Pete. You hear anything, flash them little pencil torches I gave you all. OK? Any questions?"

"Once your inside the warehouse, you won't be able to see the torches ... what then, Jimmy?" Micky asked.

"Good question, Micky. If anybody comes while we're inside, we'll hear the big doors open, so don't worry about that. Don't forget, nobody's working tonight, it's Friday remember, they didn't want anybody to see them stash the money, that's why Morris's dad ain't working."

"Oh yeah, 'course," Pete said, "I get it now, very clever them Greeks."

"Not that clever or we wouldn't be here, would we?" Bertie said laughing.

"Come on, Bertie, let's go," Jimmy grabbed his arm, "and keep behind me ... off you go, you lot, and keep your bloody eyes open."

They all went nervously to their positions.

Jimmy climbed the wall. He leant down and grabbed Bertie's arm, helping him up. They both jumped down the other side making sure they kept to the shadows. They made their way round to the back of the warehouse where the wall was higher.

"Where's that bloody ladder?" Jimmy said to Bertie as they came to the spot where they'd got up before.

"It's here, mate ... gimme a hand, will ya," Bertie said, gripping the end of the ladder.

Jimmy got the other end and together they carried it to the spot where the scaffolding poles were. Together, they pushed the heavy ladder up the side of the wall.

"Come on, up we go," Jimmy said to Bertie. "When we hit the roof, you stay up there while I go in, Bertie. I don't trust that lot's judgement watching out for anyone, all right, mate?"

Bertie nodded. "With you, Jimmy, but take care in there."

"I will."

They both scrambled up the ladder until they reached the top where the two poles went across to the warehouse roof. Jimmy reached up and grabbed hold of the scaffold poles and, arm over arm, got across.

"Come on, Bertie." Bertie grabbed hold of the poles and quickly got across to join his mate.

"It's a good job those poles are stuck in that wall, else they'd have rolled," Bertie whispered to Jimmy.

"What you whispering for? Nobody can hear you up here, mate," Jimmy said to him, laughing, "Let's get that skylight up."

They both carefully scrambled across the roof, taking care there were no holes. They reached the skylight, which came up easily as it did before. Jimmy got inside, his feet finding the steps that led down to the first floor.

"Take care, mate ... shout if you need me," Bertie said to Jimmy, giving him a pat on the shoulder.

Jimmy disappeared through the skylight, his eyes becoming

used to the dark interior. His feet finally touched the wooden floor. Looking around to get his bearings, he finally saw the big freezer down on the ground floor. He walked down the main stairs to the ground floor keeping very quiet.

"You never know," he said to himself, "there could be someone here."

He made his way over to the freezer feeling for the light switch that would illuminate the freezer. He found it and turned it on. Grabbing hold of the handle to the freezer door, Jimmy pulled it and the door opened, the cold hitting him with a rush.

Jimmy shivered as he moved into the freezer, the light piercing his eyes. He waited until he could focus again and started to look around for the carcass.

Jimmy already had the gloves on he'd brought with him. He started to go through the rows of meat before him.

"Shit," he said to himself as he came across the cow carcasses at the back of the freezer. "'Course they would be back here, too risky in the front. A nosy meat porter might find something," Jimmy mumbled to himself again.

He quickly sorted through them until he came to one which had a red mark on it. "Morris was right," he thought to himself. "This has got to be it, it's the only one with a mark." He took the knife out of his pocket, opened it and cut the stitching in the middle. Putting his hand inside, he felt about but couldn't feel anything. He pushed his arm deeper inside, and felt a lump at the bottom.

"Bingo," he said aloud. "This is it, it must be." He shook the lump about until it broke loose. Gently he lifted it out and dropped it on the floor. The ice broke off as soon as it touched the floor. A parcel covered in tape was left there as the ice fell away.

Jimmy jumped in the air. "I've fucking done it." He bent down and picked up the package. "This is it, I've bloody got it, great."

Jimmy took a bag out of his pocket, opened it up, and took some cat gut and a big needle out, which was already threaded. He looked around and saw some meat steaks over on a box. He went over and broke two off about the same size as the money package. Opening up the package with the money in, he carefully took the notes out, putting them into the bag. He then transferred the two steaks into the money bag. Taping the meat back up in the bag, he put it back into the carcass and, using the needle, sewed it back up again. He stood back and admired his work.

"When that freezes up again, they won't notice a thing," Jimmy laughed. Picking up his bag with the money, he peered round the freezer floor. "The knife, shit, the knife." He'd left it on the box with the steaks in it. He walked over, retrieved the knife, dropped it in the bag with the money. He slowly backed out of the freezer, closing the door and switching the light off.

Jimmy quickly made his way back to the first floor. He grabbed hold of the stairs and made his way up to the top.

"Bertie, you still there? Bertie ... " he tried not to shout.

"I'm here, Jimmy, I'm here." Bertie poked his head through the skylight as Jimmy reached the top.

"Take hold of the bag, Bertie." He handed it over as he came back out on to the warehouse roof.

"Wow, you got it, mate, bloody hell," Bertie said to him.

"Come on, Bertie, let's go, I don't want to push our luck too much."

They gently closed the skylight and gradually made their way back down to the ground. They lowered the ladder down and walked back to the wall where they'd climbed over.

Bertie went first, climbed up and helped Jimmy up. They both jumped back down on the roadside where Lenny and Micky were still keeping watch.

"Welcome back," Lenny said, laughing, "how'd you get on then?"

"Great. Come on, let's piss off. Where's your van? Call the others over, Bertie."

When they were all together in the back of Lenny's van, Jimmy said to them, "Meet at my place today about 8 tonight. I'll share this out then, OK, boys."

"Well done, Jimmy, and you, Bertie," they all said.

When the van stopped at Jimmy's estate, they all got out. Jimmy walked up to Lenny's van door. "I'll pay you tomorrow morning, Lenny. I'll come round about 10, all right?"

"Yeah, Jimmy, see you tomorrow," Lenny said and drove off.

"Right, lads," he looked at his watch. It was 2.30am. "I'm off, see you all later."

He looked at Bertie. "I meant to say to Lenny 'today', not 'tomorrow'. See you later," and he walked off.

Chapter 10

SERGEANT KEN SANDERS WAS SITTING IN HIS OFFICE IN THE KING'S CROSS POLICE STATION JUST OFF THE CALEDONIAN ROAD. IN A CHAIR OPPOSITE HIM SAT HIS PARTNER JOHN ROWLEY. IT WAS EARLY SATURDAY MORNING, JUST AFTER 3.00AM.

Rowley said, "Just got a report, Sarge. A gang of kids were hanging about the old warehouses round the back of the station."

"And what time was that ... I mean, when it was reported?" the Sergeant asked.

"Er, let's have a look." Sanders thumbed back through the pages. "Just after 12, Sarge."

"Oh, great, they've most probably stolen fucking King's Cross Station and all the bloody trains by now," Sergeant Sanders shouted. "I don't believe it, why weren't we informed earlier?"

"Don't know, Sarge, but I bet it was the little gang of shits we're after. What you going to do?"

Sergeant Sanders stood up. "Come on, John, let's go and have a look. I doubt if there will be anything about now but a report's got to be made out." He shrugged his shoulders. "Let's go."

As they walked out of the police station, Sergeant Sanders stopped at the front desk.

"Excuse me," he spoke to the policeman on duty, "I've got a report here about a gang of kids over at Pancras Way. Why wasn't I told at 12 when it was reported, rather than now at bloody 3? Can you explain?"

"Sorry, Sarge, whoever took the call must have mislaid the report. I only found it when I came on at 2.30." He looked lost for words.

"Forget it. Rowley and myself are going over there now to investigate it. Don't forget that, will you?" he added, the "don't forget" coming out in a big roar.

They walked out into the yard and got into their unmarked police car and drove off. In ten minutes they were at the back of the warehouse.

"Very quiet, Sarge," Rowley said. "Shall we get out or what?"

"Yeah, come on, John, let's have a quick look."

They opened the car doors and both stood beside the car.

"Blimey, it's a bit nippy for July, ain't it, Sarge?" Rowley said, stretching his arms. They walked over to the gates of the warehouse which Jimmy had just been in. The Sergeant tried the gates but they were firmly locked.

"Nobody's been in here tonight, I can tell you ... them kids wouldn't go in there, it's a bleeding store for cold meat. They wouldn't get in there anyway. Look!" he said pointing up to the side of the warehouse, "there's a camera up there. If they've been in there, the camera will have caught them. Come on, nothing here. We'll come back Monday morning. They don't have security here Friday nights so there won't be anyone here anyway."

"Here, Sarge, tell me, why don't they have security Friday nights? Funny that, don't you think?" Rowley said to his superior.

The Sergeant looked at him. "Yeah, it is funny when you think about it. I'll have to have words with the owner, might be some logical reason. Anyway, come on let's ..." he looked at his watch, "Let's go and have a sandwich and a cuppa down at the stall at King's Cross Station. We'll see if Barney Hepton, the snitch, is there. He might give us something." He looked at his partner. "How much money you got on you?"

"Er, I don't know, I'll have a look," Rowley said, putting his hand in his trouser pocket and pulling out the change.

"Not change, Detective, crinkle cabbage paper money, in case I have to give Barney anything."

"Oops, sorry Sarge." Rowley put his £3 and few pence back in his pocket and pulled out his wallet from his inside jacket pocket. He opened it and took out some notes, counting them. He looked at Sergeant Sanders.

"£38, Sarge."

"That'll do, Detective Rowley," Sanders said to him holding his hand out.

"Hang on, hang on, Sarge, ain't you got nothing?"

"Sergeants don't give bribes, their young partners do. Give it over."

Rowley reluctantly handed his money over and said, "Here, I want a receipt for this, you know."

His Sergeant looked at him, counting the money out and putting it in his pocket. He smiled and said, "I'll give it you back on Thursday out of my own pocket. OK. Now let's go and have a cuppa."

They walked back to the car, got in and drove off, John Rowley doing the driving.

"Pull in around the back of York Way and park in front of the pub over there," he said pointing in front.

Detective Rowley pulled up outside the pub, got out and waited for Sanders. When the Sergeant was finally out of the car, they walked across the road to the forecourt of the Station. The coffee stall was crowded, as usual. Mostly with prostitutes, drunks, down-and-outs and layabouts.

"You name it, it's here," Sergeant Sanders had said to Detective Rowley some time ago.

Rowley pushed his way to the front, not that he needed to. The crowd knew they were coppers so they made a path for them anyway.

"Two teas and two bacon rolls, Sid," John said to the owner, thinking to himself, "I hope my partner's paying for this."

"Here, Sarge," Rowley said, handing him his tea and bacon sarnie, "That'll be £2.50, ta."

"Thanks, John, I'll give you the money later." He bit into his roll and sipped his tea. "This is really nice, thanks. You can't beat a bacon sandwich."

"Yeah, when someone else pays for it," Rowley thought to himself.

"There he is, the snitch, see him? He's leant on the wall at the end of the road. See him, John?"

Rowley looked towards the end of the road. It was getting

lighter now and he could see better. "Yeah, I see him. Want me to fetch him, Sarge?"

"Not bloody likely, you see them people over there at the stall? If they see Barney come to us, he'll be dead by tonight. No, he's seen us, he'll walk round the back so we can pick him up. Come on," he said, throwing the rest of his sandwich away.

Rowley looked at his sandwich and tea in his hands, looked at the car and said, "Shit, my last three bloody pounds and he wants to go chasing snitches." He threw them away and got into the car.

"Right, drive slowly down the road and go into that side turning, Wharf Road or something. Pull over and wait. Switch those bloody lights off."

John pulled over into the side road, turned off the lights and engine, and waited. All of a sudden, the back door of the car opened and a voice said, "Come on then, fucking drive off."

Later, in another street, Sanders turned around in his seat and looked at the man in the back. "Hello, Barney, what's new? Got anything for me?"

"Got a bit, Mr Sanders," he said shuffling his shoulders as he spoke. "Them 16-year-old kids you were asking about. Well the main one, Jimmy Day, is a right one. Only young but a lot of people are nervous when he's about."

"Get on with it, Barney, ain't got all bloody night," Sanders said to him.

"Sorry, Sarge. Well, anyway, there's a rumour that he and his gang done the Asian kid a couple of weeks ago ... you know, the hand job."

"Yeah, go on," Sanders said again.

"Anyway, there's eight of them and he also calls in big Lenny

Mason when he needs a bit of heavy work doing. The local kids see him as a fucking James Dean, hero type."

Sanders looked at him and said, "A fucking hero, God, that's all I need, a fucking hero."

"That's not all, Mr Sanders. They reckon Big Lenny and Jimmy might be involved in that black geezer's death in King's Cross the other week."

"Oh come on, Hepton," Rowley said, "do you really think that kid is involved with the drug gangs? And Lenny Mason? He's too bloody thick."

Barney Hepton looked at them both and said, eyes half-asleep, "I'm telling you, Sarge, he's a right little bastard."

"What about tonight, Barney, anything go down tonight?"

"Don't know yet, Sarge, but will find out for you." He started to open the car door, waiting.

"Here, here's 30 quid, enjoy it. I want more on that Jimmy Day, anything you hear I've got to know. I've got a feeling he's into a lot of things and I want him. You hear me, Barney, I fucking want him and his gang."

"Right, Mr Sanders, I'll get all I can for you." Barney opened the car door and was gone.

"What you think, Sarge ... is he telling the truth or what?" Rowley asked, "Or is he feeding you crap?"

"No, he gives me good tips, all true so far and he's the best snitch in the business. Right, lets go." He looked at his watch, "It's 5.30, we're off at 6. We'll have to go and see Mr Jimmy Bloody Hero Day, see what he's got for us. Come on, John, let's get off, I'm bloody tired, its been a long night."

Chapter 11

IT WAS SATURDAY MORNING, THE LAST DAY OF JULY AND IT WAS GOING TO BE A VERY HOT DAY. JIMMY WAS LYING DOWN ON HIS BED WITH JUST HIS BOXER SHORTS ON.

"Phew," he said to himself, "its getting bloody hotter." He rolled over on to his stomach and looked across at the clock on his sidetable, it was just on 10am.

"Time to get up," he said aloud.

He got up, putting his legs over the side of the bed and sat like that for a minute. His mind wandered back to last Friday night.

"That was a nice little earner," he thought to himself, "made some money there." He had paid all the boys off, as well as big Lenny and Morris who had given him the job. "Thanks, Morris," he'd said to him, "it went down well but don't think it will be done again. The Greeks will wise up."

"Yeah, Jimmy, you did well. Blimey, wish I'd had the bottle to do things like that but I ain't and never will." He went off with a big grin on his face, saying, "I'm off West, buy a bit of gear. See you down the disco next week, Jimmy."

"Yeah, OK, Morris, be careful. Don't flash your money about. Lotta grasses about, know what I mean?"

"Yeah, I'll take care, see ya," Morris had replied.

Jimmy came back to the present. He got up from the bed, walked over to his bedroom window, opened it wide and breathed in. He was dying for a fag. He turned from the window, opened his bedroom door, walked out to the hallway and over to his dad's room. Quietly opening the door, he looked in. His bed was still made up and hadn't been slept in.

"Dirty bastard, he's next door with that scrubber Rose. He must have been pissed again." He closed the door, walked over to his brother's door and opened it. Mark was sat up in bed reading the Saturday Mirror, not that he could read very well. "Like me," Jimmy thought to himself.

He spoke to him as he sat down on his bed. "You nicked dad's paper out of the letterbox then," he said, smiling at his brother.

"The old man's not in yet, Jimmy. He's out with old Rose next door, giving her one, no doubt," he said laughing.

"Here, watch your tongue, young'un," Jimmy said, ruffling his hair. "Come on, get up then, get dressed and we'll go up the High Street. I'll treat you to some new jeans."

"Cor. Thanks, Jimmy." He jumped out of bed, eager to get going with his brother.

* * *

Sergeant Sanders looked out of the car window. "It's going to be a scorcher today, Johnny boy," he said to his partner who was munching on a burger.

"Yeah, right, Sarge, and I don't want to be stuck in this bloody car all day either, I can tell you," he said, carrying on chewing.

Sanders looked at him. "We're going up the big estate today. See if we can get to talk to that Jimmy Day. A little bird told me he's in all Saturday afternoons. His dad's usually out, there ain't a better time. What do you think?"

"Yeah, it's OK if he'll talk to you ... knowing what I've heard, he won't," replied Rowley.

"We'll see, we'll see. I don't even know what he looks like ..."
Rowley interrupted him before he could finish, pointing across the road. "It looks like you won't have to wait long to see what Jimmy Day looks like ... that's him over there with his kid brother."

Sanders sat up in his car seat. "Where ... where is he?"

"Over there, look," Rowley said, pointing again, "see the two over there near Woolworth's. The tall kid is Jimmy, the other one is his brother Mark."

"Well, well ... so that's the big hero, and only 16. Bloody hell, its unbelievable, ain't it. A kid that young can put fear into grown men and women and look at him, he looks about 18, never mind 16. How did you know him, Detective?"

"Well, Sarge, I picked his dad up one night, me and Constable Brown. The old geezer was causing a stir down The George pub. Anyway, to cut it short, we took him home and his boys, Jimmy and Mark, came to the door and fetched him in. Never really got talking to the boys, though."

"Right, come on," the Sergeant said to his partner, "out the car, let's see what they're up to, if anything."

They both got out of the car, locked it and started off down the High Street after Jimmy and Mark.

Jimmy glanced across the road and saw the two men. He knew they were coppers, it was that obvious. He laughed to himself.

"What you laughing at, Jimmy?" Mark asked him, looking around.

"Nothing, bruv, nothing. Come on, let's go and have a look down the market ... some of the shops are good down there. Mind you, some of them are crap as well.

Jimmy walked on knowing that the coppers were following him. He would get Mark's jeans, get him his usual hamburger and chips, then he'd have to lose these two Old Bill.

Jimmy had taken a £1,000 out with him today; if the cops happened to stop him, they might do a body search on him like they do, then he'd be right up the creek, "'Cause I ain't got an answer as to why I'm carrying so much," he said to himself.

Rowley looked at Sanders and said, "You think he's made us, Sarge?" looking a bit worried.

"Na, he ain't got the intelligence to spot us ... come on, keep walking."

"In here, Mark," Jimmy said to his brother. They were now in Camden Lock Market. "This is quite a good one," Jimmy said as they went into one shop. Jimmy looked casually around, and saw the coppers about a 100 yards away.

The shop was crowded with tourists and locals. Jimmy looked at his brother and said, "What do you want ... Levi's, Mark?"

"Think so, Jimmy," his brother said. He looked round. "I'll see what they've got anyway."

Mark picked out some jeans after a while. A little while later, his brother said to him, "Look, Mark, I've got to shoot home for a minute. Here's a tenner, nip into Mac's, get what you want. I'll be back in about half-an-hour, all right? Wait for me there, OK?"

Mark took the money. "All right, Jimmy, don't be too long, will ya?"

"No, 'course I won't, silly. Look, do me a favour. Nip out that side door, go over round the back of the market and come back near the bridge. Don't ask me why, just do it. See you later."

Jimmy watched his brother exit through the side door and disappear into the crowd. Jimmy went to the main door, looked out, and saw the coppers across the road, leaning against a wall.

"What a couple of prats," Jimmy said out loud. He walked further into the shop which was quite large and stepped out the side door, like his younger brother had just done.

"Come on, John," Sergeant Sanders said to his partner, "they've been in there over half-an-hour. They might do a moody. Let's go."

They walked across the street which was heaving with bodies. Detective Rowley was a little distracted by the young women and was nearly knocked over by a bike.

"Stop bloody ogling the women, for God's sake. You're on bloody duty, remember. You're like a bloody kid eyeing up a jar of sweets."

"Sorry, Sarge, can't help but look now and then," he said smiling.

They were outside the shop by then. Sanders was just about to go into the shop when a young couple stopped him.

"Excuse me, mister, spare a pound? We ain't eaten for two days and we're starving."

Sanders looked at them; they were well dressed but smelt. The young guy was carrying a can of beer, the girl with him was smoking.

"Fuck off ... if you can afford to buy beer and fags you ain't starving in my book." He looked around, pulling his police ID out of his pocket. He showed it to the young couple and said, "Get lost or I'll run you in for begging. Now piss off."

The couple walked away but not before the young man had put two fingers up and shouted to the policeman, "Dirty pig."

"Bloody nerve," Rowley said, "want me to get him, Sarge?"

"No, not really, Rowley. We're on a job, remember." He shook his head. "Come on, in the bloody shop."

Sanders knew as soon as he entered the shop that Jimmy Day was long gone. "Right, come on, round his bloody flat. He's got something to hide or he wouldn't have run. He must have spotted us when we were talking to them two outside."

* * *

Jimmy opened his front door and walked in carefully, putting the safety chain on behind him. "Anybody here?" he shouted. He thought his old man might be in, but no response. He quickly walked into his bedroom and took out the wad of money he had stashed in his inside jacket pocket. He tossed it down on the bed. Walking to the head of the bed, he pulled it away, knelt down and lifted up a section of the wallpaper. Behind it was a small door in the wall. Jimmy took a key out of his pocket and inserted it into the door. He opened it and retrieved a box from inside. He got up and walked back to the end of the bed, putting the box on it. He picked up the money, counted out £100, and put the remainder into the box. He took it back to the wall and put it into the safe, locked it, put the key back in his pocket and pushed the bed back. He stood away from the bed and looked at the spot where the little safe was.

"You'd never know it was there," he said out loud. "Big Lenny did a good job for me there." He smiled and walked out of the bedroom. As he walked into the hallway, he heard the phone ring. It rang three times, stopped and rang again.

"Bertie," he said to himself. He walked into the living room and picked the phone up.

"Hello, Bertie, what's new?" Jimmy said down the phone.

"Hi, Jimmy," Bertie said, his Irish brogue coming through strongly, "you coming out?"

"Yeah, 'course I am, mate." Jimmy went on to tell him about the coppers and how he had had to rush home.

"Blimey, you were lucky. The copper you describe sounds like Sergeant Sanders, Scotch bastard. Thinks he's Sherlock Holmes and his dopey partner Detective Rowley, who thinks Shrove Tuesday is a football team. If they'd got you, they'd have searched you down to your socks. Dead lucky, mate, dead lucky. Look, I'll meet you downstairs in five minutes. OK? "

"How do you know them coppers then, Bertie?" he said.

"I don't know them ... my dad's had a run in with 'em quite a few times when he's been pissed."

Having met up, they were walking out of the estate, crossing the road into the High Street, when Bertie stopped. "Don't look now, Jimmy, but guess who's coming towards us."

* * *

Detective Rowley and Sergeant Sanders made their way back to the unmarked police car. As they approached it, Rowley turned to Sanders and said, "Shit, we've only got a bleeding parking ticket. I don't believe it," he said, kicking the car in rage. "Some day, this is."

Sanders looked at his partner. "Leave it, let's walk, come on."

They started to walk away from the car towards the big estate at the end of the High Street. As they rounded the bend at the end of the road, Sanders tapped his partner on the shoulder. "Well would you believe it ... it must be luck," he said pointing up the road, "Jimmy Day ... and look who he's with, Bertie Paddy O'Cooney. I've been up his house a few times."

"What you going to do, Sarge. Pull 'em over?" Rowley asked.

"No, not now. Another day will do. Not while he's with someone. Come on, let's get back to the station." They turned and walked back to the car.

Jimmy looked down the road at the two coppers. "Fuck," he said to Bertie. "Now what?"

"Nothing, mate, it looks like they're going, heading back to the car. Bollocks to 'em. Come on, let's cross over and go and get Mark," he said looking at Jimmy.

"Not before I've had a big burger. Come on, ignore them bastards."

As Sanders and Rowley got back into the car, Jimmy and Bertie walked by. Jimmy's arm went behind his back and he stuck two fingers up in the air. Turning his head, he mouthed to them, "Up yours, copper."

Chapter 12

"BERTIE, BERTIE, GET TO THE PHONE, IT'S JIMMY. HURRY UP, HE AIN'T GOT ALL DAY," MR COONEY WAS SHOUTING OUTSIDE HIS SON'S DOOR. HE SHARED HIS BEDROOM WITH HIS TWO BROTHERS, SEAN AND PADDY, BOTH YOUNGER THAN HIM.

"Coming, Dad," Mr Cooney heard him shout from the other side of the door, "I'm up, I'm up."

It was Friday morning, a week after the fracas with the coppers. The night before, the gang had all gone down into West End and had got into a fight with some blokes down from Scotland. They were much older than Jimmy's gang but Jimmy and his pals had fought back until they had to make a run for it. Dave Smith had slashed one of the men with his knife, nearly cutting the bloke's finger off; that was another good reason to scarper.

Bertie came out of the bedroom rubbing his eyes. "Blimey,

Dad, what time is it?"

"Its after 11," his dad said, looking at him, "are your brothers awake yet?"

"Yeah, Dad, they're playing on their computer."

Bertie walked into the kitchen and picked up the phone. "Hello, Jimmy, what's new?"

"Hi, Bertie," Jimmy said, "some bloody night, wasn't it?"

"Sure was, mate. Lucky we got away, they'd have killed us, fucking Scotch bastards." Bertie laughed as he spoke. "On our own turf, we'd have had 'em."

"I don't think so, mate," Jimmy interrupted, "anyway, I rang to tell you that Dave was picked up by the Old Bill last night. Someone must have seen the blood on his clothes and phoned the cops. They took him over to West End Central nick. I phoned this morning to his house but his mum told me to piss off and slamed the phone down. I'll phone or talk to his dad later."

"Bloody hell, Jimmy, what we going to do?" Bertie said.

Jimmy laughed "They ain't got nothing on us, mate. Hurry up, get dressed and come on over. It's my birthday tomorrow, I'm bloody 17. Do the town tomorrow, mate. Anyway, hurry up," and he put the phone down.

* * *

Bertie knocked on Jimmy's door. It was just after 12pm. Bertie was sweating; the lifts had broken down and he'd had to walk up 18 floors to Jimmy's landing. The door was opened by Jimmy's dad.

"Morning, Mr Day," Bertie said. "Jimmy in?"

"Yeah, come in, he's in his bedroom, go straight through."

"Mark away, Mr Day?" Bertie asked as he walked in.

"Yeah, won't be back until September. He's decided he wants to stay with his sister until school starts. Went on the train yesterday."

Bertie went straight up to Jimmy's bedroom door and knocked.

"Come in," Jimmy shouted out. Bertie walked in to see Jimmy lying on his bed, arms behind his head; fully dressed.

"Watcha, mate, you ready to go?" Bertie said to him.

"All the way, mate, all the way." Jimmy swung his legs off the bed and stood up. "Listen, Bertie, before we go out, I want you to phone up Dave's place, see if he's home or not. Don't tell his mum and dad you're with me. Just ask if Dave's all right and what's the score. You know where the phone is ... I'm gonna have a bacon sarnie, you want one?"

"Er ... all right, didn't have time to have breakfast this morning," Bertie said, smiling at his mate, "didn't get up until 11."

Jimmy was putting the bacon sandwiches on a plate when Bertie came back into the kitchen. He looked at Jimmy, his face as white as a sheet.

"Did you get hold of him, mate? Is Dave home yet?" Jimmy looked at Bertie. "You OK, mate? You look like you've seen a ghost. Too many late nights. Here's your sarnie, sit down, want a cup of t..."

Bertie interrupted him, "It's Dave, Jimmy ... he's fucking dead. Them coppers killed him." The tears started to flow from his already red eyes.

"WHAT? What you fucking saying? DEAD? He can't be dead."

"The cops have killed him Jimmy, his ... his mum told me they found him in the ... the ..." Bertie was still crying, trying to wipe his eyes with his sleeve, which made it harder to speak.

"In the fucking where, Bertie?" Jimmy said grabbing hold of his friend. "Pull yourself together, mate, pull yourself together, and tell me. In the where?"

Bertie wiped his eyes and looked at his mate. "His mum said the cops found him hanging in his cell. The door wasn't even locked, they just put him in there while they were discussing what to do with him. That's all she told me. His dad's down the nick ... she's waiting to go back down ... there's a woman cop with her."

"Jesus, I don't believe it, them bastards, why would he hang himself? Why? He was only in as a suspect, nothing else. They must have done something to him, bet your bloody life on it. Come on, let's go."

They both walked out of the kitchen and into the hallway. Jimmy's dad was sat in the living room drinking a cup of tea. "Dave Smith's dead," Jimmy said to his dad. "They reckon he hanged himself down at the nick."

His dad looked at him startled. "You're kidding me, ain't ya?" he said.

"No, he ain't, Mr Day. His mum just told me on the phone," Bertie said.

"Bloody hell." Jimmy's dad looked shaken. "How the hell can that happen?" he asked, looking at his son. "What you think, Jimmy?"

Jimmy didn't speak to his dad a lot, but this was an exception. He said, "I think they provoked him, scared him ... made him so frightened that he killed himself, but I'll find out somehow, you wait and see."

"You keep out of it, Jimmy, this is above your head. Keep out of it, let his family sort it," his dad said.

"They can sort it, but I'll fucking finish it, you'd better believe it. Come on, Bertie, let's blow, get some information off the streets."

As they wandered outside, Bertie turned to Jimmy. "Look, Jimmy, your dad is most probably right. Let his family sort it, they won't want you around. His mother hates you with a vengeance ... why, I don't know."

Jimmy looked at his friend. "Look, mate, some things you don't understand. Here," they were near a bench at a bus stop, "sit down a minute, Bertie."

Sitting, Jimmy said, "You remember when Dave had that party at their flat last year for his mum?"

"Yeah ... what's that got to do with her hating you?" Bertie said looking at him.

"Well, his mum tried to come on to me. She was a bit pissed, but not that pissed. You remember they ran out of booze. I offered to go and get some. Well, she came with me, remember?"

"Yeah, now I think about it, she did go with you. It took you about an hour ... now I know why."

Jimmy laughed. "Yeah, nothing went on, believe me. When we got down to the ground floor and came out of the lift, she told me she fancied me and tried to kiss me. Grabbed hold of my cock, said she could do with a good screw there and then. I told her not to be so stupid, but she kept on. I told her to fuck off and called her an old scrubber. Said she ought to be ashamed of herself. With that, she smacked me round the face and stormed off."

"That's right," Bertie said, "she never came back until later. I remember, you came back by yourself. Nobody noticed her not coming back, 'cause everyone was pissed. Where did she go then?"

"She went round her husband's best mate's flat. He's been screwing her for years."

"So that's why she hates you ... well, well, well."

"Yeah, that and thinking that I was leading her son astray.

Fucking cheek, the old cow," Jimmy said.

"What we going to do about poor old Dave, Jimmy?"

"Leave it, Bertie, leave it. I'll find out later what the true story is. Come on, I've got to tell the rest of the boys."

Chapter 13

"YOU MEAN TO TELL ME THAT THE BOY HAS BLOODY HANGED HIMSELF?" SERGEANT SANDERS BARKED AT THE DESK POLICEWOMAN WHO WAS ON DUTY AT WEST CENTRAL. "YOU'VE GOT TO BE FUCKING JOKING. HE WAS ALL RIGHT TWO HOURS AGO, I DON'T BELIEVE IT. CHRIST, WHAT A BLOODY MESS. JESUS, GOD!"

Sanders' mind went back to the previous night when he'd received a phonecall from West End Central Police saying that they had picked up a young lad whose clothes were covered in blood.

"Sorry, Sergeant, but the address the lad gave us seems to be in your manor ... thought you might want a word with him. Won't say a thing, only his name and address ... David Smith," the policewoman had told him.

"David Smith ... about 17, you say? Hold on, I'll be down in half-an-hour." He'd shouted to his partner, "John, come on, mate, might be the break we need on this young gang."

"What's up Sarge?" his partner asked him, "we got something?"

Sanders looked at him, "West Central have got Dave Smith in custody, found him wondering around Euston Road covered in blood, would you believe? Come on, let's go."

By the time they arrived at the West End Police Station, it was just after 1am on Saturday morning. They walked up to the reception desk; Sanders took out his ID, and showed it to the constable on duty. "Here to see Inspector Cline ... its about the young lad brought in, David Smith, is the Inspector about?"

The constable looked at their IDs. "Go in the door at the end of the passage way," he said, pointing to his left. "The Inspector's in there having a cuppa, Sarge."

"Thanks," Sanders said to him. "Come on, John, let's see what we've got." Sanders had pushed his way through the swing door, which was labelled "Charge Room".

Inspector Cline was sitting at the end of a long table. On one side stood a young policewoman and at the other end of the table sat Dave Smith. He was smoking a cigarette, given to him, no doubt, by the Inspector.

"Hello, Inspector," Sanders said to him. "I'm Sergeant Ken Sanders ..." and he nodded to John Rowley, "and this is my partner, Detective Rowley."

"Pleased to meet you both. Well, this is the young lad, know him?"

"Yeah, I know him. Can we have a word with him, Inspector?"

Inspector Cline stood up, beckoning to the Sergeant to follow him out of the room. When they were outside, the Inspector said, "You can have a word with him, but I can tell you he's given us nothing. Said he'd been in a fight down Soho. We have had no reports of anybody hurt or of any fights, so we'll have to let him go soon and as he's only 16 we don't want to hold him too long, if you know what I mean."

"Thanks, Inspector, I just want to ask him a few things, won't be long."

"OK, he's all yours Sergeant. I'll tell the policewoman she can go now." He walked back in the room with Sanders.

The Inspector looked at Dave and said, "Looks like someone knows you, David. The Sergeant wants a word with you." The Inspector looked at Sanders. "All yours. I'm going home. Come on, Constable, let's go."

When they had gone, Sanders sat down facing Dave. "Well, David, it looks like we meet again."

Dave 'Mack the Knife' Smith looked at Sanders. He felt very scared and vulnerable, nowhere near as confident as he did when he was with the gang and Jimmy. The Sargeant looked at him, just staring, not saying anything, testing Dave's nerves.

"Where did you get the blood from, David?" Sanders finally asked him.

"I got it in a fight down the West End. I've already told the other copper that," Dave said nervously.

Sergeant Sanders looked at him. "What happened to the other guy? Cut his head, did you? Wonder where all the blood came from," he said smirking.

"Don't remember, Sergeant. He must have cut himself … there was about 30 of them and only eight of us," Dave said, "and them Scottish bastards were throwing bottles at us."

Sanders stood up and said to his partner, "Outside a minute, John."

Outside the door, he said, "Look, phone up University

College Hospital and Middlesex Hospital, find out if anyone has been in with a bad cut or something. Fast as you can, and tell the hospital it might have happened beween 11 and 1 in the morning, OK?"

"Right, Sarge, I'm right on it."

It was just after 2am when his partner came back. Detective Rowley poked his head around the door. "Sarge, a minute."

When they were outside, Rowley said, "Good thinking, Sarge, you were right. Some blokes from Scotland came into the UCH Casualty at 11.30 last night. One of them, a James McLinden, had half his thumb hanging off. He's OK, though. They sewed it back on according to the doctor I spoke to. McLinden said he was attacked by a gang of youths with knives and other things."

"Nice one, John ... lets go and put the frighteners on David Smith. Go and get a couple of teas and get Smith a can of Coke or something."

Sanders sat back down opposite Smith, whose eyes were starting to glaze over. "Now, Smith, you didn't tell us all the story, did you? We know about the knifing ... who did the cutting, you or your buddies, or was it your big hero, Jimmy Day?"

He looked at his partner, then back to Dave. "The guy you or your mates stabbed is very ill in hospital. He's lost a lot of blood and there are witnesses to say that they saw you stab him once. Did you all stab him as well? You're in big fucking trouble, David. You won't get out of this one, my boy. Do you hear me? Do you hear, me boy? You'll get sent down for this and they love fresh meat like you in the nick."

"I ... I ... only cut him once. I was only trying to defend my ... "

"But you nearly killed the poor sod, he's bleeding to death in there. Who did it, David? Was it you or are you defending your mate, Jimmy Day? 'Cause if you are, you're going down for a long time, I can tell you that. Now out with it, lad, who are you defending, or was it you?"

Sanders banged his fists on the table. He looked at David Smith, anger in his eyes, and said to him, "I want to know about last night and I also want to know about the Asian kid your gang fucking mutilated and anything else you have in that bloody pea brain of yours … and if you don't, I'm going to throw the fucking book at you.

"I'll also get word to your bloody gang that you grassed them up. You know what Jimmy Day will do to you, don't you, you fucking worm? Have you been listening to me, you fucking shit, have you? Do you want to spend your bloody life in the slammer? You will, believe me."

David Smith looked at the Sergeant, then at his partner, tears were streaming down his face and he was shaking uncontrollably. "Please, please, I can't grass my mates. I can't do that … I wanna go home to my mum and dad. I wanna go home." Looking at Rowley, David pleaded, "Please ask him to let me go home."

Rowley looked at the boy and thought to himself, "Ease up, Sarge, you're going too bloody far."

"Sarge, can I have a word?"

Sanders looked at him. "OK." He looked at David Smith and said, "Make your mind up, boy, you ain't got long."

Outside the room, Sanders looked at his partner. "Well, John, what's up?"

"Don't you think you're going a bit strong, Ken? Bleeding to death and all that … what's that all about? You've got the kid frightened out of his mind. You can't do that."

Sanders looked at him. "Are you bloody kidding me, John? These bloody kids are animals … are you going soft on me or what?"

"No, I'm not, but I can't let you bully the boy, it's wrong and you know it is."

"Look, I'll do whatever I've got to do to get a confession out of him. Do you think he cared about the guy he stabbed, and what about the Asian kid? He's lost his fucking hand for god's sake. Where you been, Detective? Right, I'm going to give him a couple of hours by himself in a cell, that will loosen his tongue. Come on."

They went back into the room. Dave Smith was still shaking but he'd stopped crying. Sanders sat down again, opposite the boy and said to him, "Right, David, I'm going to leave you for a couple of hours, give you time to think things over. When I come back, I want it all on paper, all of it, and remember … you let me down and you're in fucking serious trouble. You hear me, David?"

Dave Smith looked at him; he was really scared, didn't know which way to turn. He started to cry again and, trying to talk, said, "Please, can I go home? Please …" he begged.

Sanders looked at him with contempt and said, "You can go home when you've given me all the names. I want them written down and signed. Then you can go." He looked at his partner. "Take him to one of the cells, John. Tell the desk constable not to lock the cell door and to look in on him while we're away. Hurry up, I'm fucking starving."

Chapter 14

SANDERS' MIND WAS JOLTED BACK TO THE PRESENT. HE STOOD LOOKING AT THE POLICEWOMAN. HE COULDN'T BELIEVE WHAT HE WAS HEARING. LOOKING AT THE WPC, HE SAID TO HER AGAIN, "HOW CAN HE BE DEAD? WE LEFT HIM HERE WITH YOUR DESK OFFICER. HE WAS SUPPOSED TO LOOK IN ON THE LAD EVERY TEN MINUTES.

"WHAT BLOODY HAPPENED?" SANDERS SPUN ROUND, LOOKING AT HIS PARTNER JOHN ROWLEY. HE SAID TO HIM, "CAN YOU BELIEVE THIS, ROWLEY. WHAT'S GOING ON HERE?"

By the time he had finished talking, the police reception area was a mass of bodies, each trying to see what was going on.

WPC Shaw tried to talk to the Sergeant above the noise. "Sargeant, the constable who was on duty at 2am took the boy, David Smith, a cup of tea and a sandwich at approximately 3.30am. He found the boy hanging by his coat belt which had been tied to the window catch. The catch was made of heavy metal, strong enough to hold the body. The constable ran to fetch the police surgeon who was on duty at that time, but nothing could be done for the deceased. The doctor tried everything he could – heart massage, mouth to mouth – but the boy was already dead."

WPC Shaw began to cry as she carried on betwen sobs, "The doctor cut the body down with the help of Constable Deer and he was taken to UCH in Gower Street. His body will be held there until the postmortem's held," she continued to cry softly. "Constable Deer and Doctor Irvin are with Chief Inspector Jones trying to explain what happened." She dried her eyes with a handkerchief and walked out into the adjourning office where her sobbing could still be heard.

"Poor girl, it must be tough for her, she's only been at this nick two days," someone in the room said.

"What the hell is going on here?"

Everyone spun round. The Chief Inspector came into the reception area, closely followed by Dr Irvin and the constable.

"Come on, come on, back to your bloody duties. Its not a bloody circus," he shouted.

The Chief walked up to Sanders and asked, "Are you Sergeant Sanders?"

"Yes, Sir. And this is my assistant Detective Rowley."

"Right, come with me. What a bloody mess," he said, walking back into his office behind the reception desk. "Not you, Detective Rowley, you stay out here until I call you."

"Right, Sir," Rowley answered, going out and closing the door behind him.

The Chief sat down at his desk, looked at the man standing in front of him and said, "Sit down, Sergeant Sanders."

Sanders sat down facing the Chief.

"Now, Sanders, what the hell happened out there this morning? And I want the bloody truth."

After Sanders had told him about the night's events, the Chief looked at him, pausing a moment. "Why did he hang himself? Did you put pressure on him, Sergeant. Did you threaten him? If you did, your're in deep bloody trouble, I can tell you that."

"Sir, I didn't put any pressure on the lad. I've no idea why he hanged himself. It's very tragic, Sir, and I'm deeply sorry for his family."

"I bet you bloody are," the Chief thought to himself.

"Right, Sargeant, send your assistant in and be around if I want you."

* * *

Detective Rowley sat in front of the desk, twiddling his thumbs. The Chief was saying to him, "So you have nothing more to tell me then, Detective? Nothing you could have missed?"

"Not a thing, Sir ... Sargeant Sanders was quite soft on him, didn't put any pressure on him at all. That's all I can tell you Sir."

"OK, Rowley, you can go, but be around because I might need you again today."

Later, as they were driving back to King's Cross Police Station, Rowley turned to Sergeant Sanders. "I didn't drop you in it Sarge, if that's what you're thinking. I just told him you were a bit soft on him and had no idea why he'd hang himself."

Sanders looked at him, worried. "We are in deep shit, believe me," he said.

"Hang on, hang on, Sarge … I didn't do anything at all to the boy. Remember, I told you to go easy on him," Rowley said.

"If I get dropped in it, Johnny boy, you will, too. You remember that, laddie," Sanders said looking at him. "And don't you fucking forget it, either."

Chapter 15

THE PARTY WAS IN FULL SWING DOWN AT THE GEORGE PUB. JIMMY HAD HIRED THE BACK ROOM FOR HIS SEVENTEENTH BIRTHDAY.

"Are you sure you're doing the right thing, Jimmy?" Bertie said to him as they walked into the pub. "Dave's only been dead a bloody day and we're having a party."

"He would have wanted me to have it, believe me," Jimmy said to him. "Don't worry about it, Bertie. You hear any more about the death or anything at all?"

Bertie looked at him.

"Hang on a minute ... let me get a drink for us both and I'll tell you what my dad said. Sit down in the corner, over there away from the others. I won't be a minute."

Bertie came back with two vodkas and lemons.

"Got you a double, mate," he said to Jimmy. "Pete is pissed and so is Micky. He's chatting up that Linda."

"Cheers, mate," Jimmy said, having a sip of his drink, "got a nice suprise for her tonight. So what's the latest on Dave?"

"Well, my dad phoned up Mr Smith this afternoon and he told him that the copper who was questioning Dave reckoned that Dave was in the clear. This copper was about to let him go when a Sergeant Sanders from King's Cross nick came down with his side-kick and from the time that bastard appeared something changed in Dave.

"He must have been terrified of something and he was fucking tough for his age. That cop must have scared him so much he just freaked out."

Jimmy hit the table with his fist. "The bastard. I'll find out what happened, just you bloody wait. That copper did it, I'll fucking get him."

"Calm down, Jimmy, we've got plenty of time to get revenge on that bastard. Look who's just come in – big Lenny," Bertie said trying to get off the subject.

"Lenny, Lenny, over here," Jimmy shouted to him.

Lenny put his hand up and shouted back, "Be over in a mo ... getting a drink first."

He came over and shook hands with Jimmy. "Happy birthday, mate." He handed over a little package. "Here, that's for you."

Lenny shook hands with Bertie, too, saying, "Hello, mate, you get bigger every time I see you. Sorry to hear about poor Dave. Any information yet?"

"Yeah, a bit," Jimmy said to him bitterly, "I'll get it sorted one way or another. Anyway, what we got here?" He started to open the package that Lenny had given him. Jimmy took the paper off and opened the box; inside was a pearl-handled flick-knife.

"Wow, Lenny, brilliant! This is great. I thought you couldn't get these any-more." He opened the blade out and waved it across in front of him. "I'd like to give this to that copper if he did that to Dave."

"Yeah, well, put it away, Jimmy" Lenny said to him. "A lot of eyes about, know what I mean?"

"Sure." Jimmy put the knife in his pocket and left the empty box on the table. He looked at Lenny. "Thanks, mate, this is a great present." They shook hands.

"Right then, Bertie, let's have a great time. How much did you give the landlord?"

"Gave him 300 up front. How many's here?" He looked around. "About 50 people. It should last a while. He'll let me know when it runs out. His missus has made loads of grub for later as well."

"Okay, what's the time?" He looked at his watch, it was just after 10.30pm. "About 12.30 we're all going back to my place," Jimmy said to them both. "My old man's staying at his fancy woman's house. My brother's still up with my sister in Manchester so the place is ours." He looked at Lenny. "You coming over, Lenny?"

"Sorry, Jimmy, my wife wants me home at 11. Some other time, though. Come on then, let's have a good drink?"

"Jimmy, Jimmy, happy birthday" Linda said, staggering over. "I thought you were going to be with me tonight. Wanna dance?" She started to giggle. "Come on ... you don't know what you're missing." She went round to Jimmy's side of the table but tripped over Lenny's foot which sent her flying on to the floor, dress up over her thighs, knickers showing. She tried to get up but kept slipping on the beer-sodden floor.

Jimmy looked at her mates and said to one of them, "Sandra, get her up, will you, and don't give her any-more booze tonight, all right."

"All right, Jimmy," she smiled at him, "see you later," as she helped Linda up. They walked and staggered away to the other side of the room where all their mates were.

The night wore on and soon it was midnight. "Come on, you lot, time to go," Johnny Mack said to the now well-pissed crowd. "Come on, come on, come on." He walked over to where Jimmy was now standing with his mates.

Jimmy shook hands with him saying, "Thanks, Johnny, you got all your money all right?"

"Yeah, thanks, Jimmy, my missus has packed all the sandwiches in the bags for you and all the booze is ready to take when you go."

"Thanks a lot for tonight, Johnny, its been a great night and everyone behaved." Jimmy turned to his mates. "Right, let's get over to my place."

"Paul, Micky and Sammy grab a hand, get the booze, and get them birds to bring the food. Look here's my keys, I'll see you up there, OK?"

The crowd was loud and boisterous as Jimmy and Bertie reached the eighteenth floor. Jimmy's door was wide open, people were milling around the balcony drinking and eating. One couple were pressed up against the wall screwing. Jimmy looked again; it was Micky giving Linda one. She could hardly stand.

"How the hell he's fucking her, beats me, Bertie. Come on, let's have a drink."

As he entered the flat, they all started to sing "Happy Birthday" to him. He put his hands up. "Thanks, everyone, who's going to get me a drink, then?"

Sally Mullens brought him over a cold beer and gave him a kiss on the lips. "Here, handsome, happy birthday."

Jimmy put his arms around her. "Thanks, Sal," and he thought to himself, "I'd love to give you one."

"My Jimmy, my Jimmy," Linda came back into the flat, closely followed by Micky. She was trying to pull her dress down which was caught in her knickers. Jimmy pulled her to one side and said, "I've got a bet with your mate, Sally. She reckons she can screw more blokes in one night than you. Is the bet on, Linda, or are you chicken?"

"If you want me to, Jimmy, I'll do it." She hiccuped twice and nearly fell over. Jimmy guided her over to his bedroom. "Get your clothes off and get on the bed."

An hour later, of all the boys or men in the room – about fifteen of them – only two hadn't fucked Linda. They were Jimmy and Bertie. By 4am, the party was over. Jimmy was in his brother's bed with Sally Mullens.

Bertie was in Jimmy's dad's with Carol Bates, a right goer from Kentish Town. He hadn't touched her, too pissed. The front room floor was covered in bodies, accompanied by a symphony of snoring, farting and God knows whatever other noises.

Linda had just pushed the last bloke off her. She was wide awake. She had more sperm in her than a killer whale. She looked around Jimmy's room but couldn't see him. Linda pushed herself off the bed and put her knickers and dress back on. She staggered over to the big mirror, looked at herself, turned around and walked out into the hallway and into the living room.

"Fucking hell," she said out loud as she stepped over the sleeping bodies, "what a bloody mess."

Her mates were all laid out with boys, half-naked. She looked around for Jimmy. No sign of him. She walked back into the hallway and opened the first door she came to. Bertie was lying there in the bed naked; the girl was Carol Bates. "Old scrubber," Linda said.

She walked along to the next door and opened it. It was the bathroom. Micky 'The Ferret' was lying in the bath, snoring. Lying on his back on the bathroom floor was Jackie 'Sweeney' Todd. He was naked from the waist down, his dick sticking up in the air. "Yuk," Linda said and closed the door.

She opened the last door. The bed under the window was lit by a beam of light coming from the lamp on the bed-side table. Jimmy was lying there naked, and next to him was her best mate, Sally Mullins, who was also naked.

"You dirty bastard, Jimmy fucking Day, and you, Sally. You bastards," She started crying, turned round and walked out of the room. "Bastards," she shouted, slamming the door as she went.

Back in the living room, one of her mates was up. "Hello, Linda, what's the time?"

Linda looked at her. "Oh, hello, Jane." She looked at her watch. "You coming home or what?"

"Yeah, Linda, wait up. What a night! You enjoyed yourself, didn't you? Didn't know you had it in you."

Linda looked at her. "What do you mean, 'Didn't know you had it in you?'"

Jane burst out laughing. "Well, you had it in you all right, time and time again," she said and burst out laughing again. She went on to tell her what had happened last night, about the so-called bet she had with Sally.

Linda started to cry. "I never made no bet, but I bet I know who did. The fucking bastard. I'll get my fucking own back on him, you wait. Come on, let's piss off." They both walked out of the flat without looking back, with Linda still sobbing.

Chapter 16

IT WAS A WEEK AFTER DAVE SMITH'S DEATH. HIS BODY HAD BEEN RELEASED TO HIS MUM AND DAD SO THEY COULD BURY HIM. THE FUNERAL TOOK PLACE ON THE MONDAY AFTER THE BODY HAD BEEN RELEASED. THE POST MORTEM REVEALED THAT DAVE HAD DIED OF A BROKEN NECK CAUSED BY HANGING.

None of the gang, led by Jimmy Day, had been invited to the funeral.

Dave's mother blamed his death on Jimmy Day. She had said, "If it wasn't for Jimmy Day and his gang, my boy would be alive today ... I have nothing but hate for them."

Jimmy gave Dave's dad £1000 for his son's funeral. He had said to Jimmy, "Really sorry, Jimmy, I don't blame you, I blame that bastard copper, he had it in for my Dave."

"Don't worry about him, Mr Smith, I'll take care of that scumbag you wait and see. Take the money, it's the least I can do."

Mr Smith looked at him. "I found a couple of thousand under Dave's mattress, Jimmy. He must have saved it somehow." He grinned. "Or a fairy godmother gave it to him. Thanks, Jimmy, see you later and don't worry about the missus. She's OK."

* * *

By the end of August, the anger over the death of David Smith had eased but had not been forgotten. The boys were sitting in the back of The George pub. It was Wednesday afternoon, not quite so hot as it had been.

"Jimmy," Johnny Mac, the landlord, called out, "phone, mate, it's Sally."

Jimmy stood up and walked over to the bar. He took the phone from Johnny. "Thanks," he said and picked up the receiver. "Yeah, what you want, Sally? Thought you were at work and I told you not to phone me here, didn't I?"

"I know you did, Jimmy and I am at work but it's important."

"What's so important ... you ain't pregnant, are you?" he smirked.

"No, I bloody ain't. Its about Dave's mum and dad. They've gone, moved out, their flat's empty."

"What! I only saw old man Smith last week," Jimmy said.

"Well, they've gone. Linda told me that her mum's a friend of Dave's mum and she phoned her yesterday and told her that she had moved. Moved out in the night, she said. What about that then?"

"Blimey, right surprised I am, Sally, I can tell ya. I wonder where they've gone?"

"Look, Jimmy, I've got to go. The boss has just come back in from lunch. See you later," she said and the line went dead.

"Thanks, Johnny." Jimmy handed the phone back over the bar, went back to his mates and explained to them what Sally had told him.

"I bet they've gone to the States," Micky piped up.

"Na, Ireland. Dave's mum was Irish," Bertie said, "back to the old country, that's where they've gone, you'll see."

"Rubbish," Pete said. "I bet they've moved over to Ealing, that's where Dave's gran lived."

Jimmy looked at them all and said, "Who gives a fuck where they've gone?" He turned around to the bar and shouted over to Johnny, "Same again, Johnny, but give Pete a glass of milk." They all laughed.

"You get that money off that camera man at the weekend, Paul? I don't see any of it."

"Yeah, mate, I gave it to Bertie, he said you'd get it off him."

Bertie looked at Jimmy. "Shit, I clean forgot with everything going on. He dipped into his inside pocket and brought out an envelope. Here, mate, sorry."

Jimmy took the envelope and opened it. "Any more to come in? Sammy, you done the gay guy. Jackie, what about the Asian shopkeeper?"

Both of them threw over envelopes, which Jimmy put into his pocket. "Right, listen, I met a couple of girls down West Monday night. They come down here three days a week from Birmingham, thick as shit, but they could earn a few bob for us. Anyway, they asked me to get them a pad over this way, and if I could protect them. Know what I mean? They're both right scrubbers and most of their clients are Arabs. Big money."

Paul shouted over, "They fuck anything, dirty bastards."

"Anyway," Jimmy went on, "I've told them to work St John's Wood, Hampstead. Plenty of money there so I'm going to get cards done. You know, stick em in phone booths ..."

"Yeah, good thinking, Jimmy," Paul said to him, "I'll put them in there."

"Anyway, we'll skip that for the moment. Listen, we're not getting any richer, so all of you think of some more scams we can get into, OK?"

They all agreed with him, finished their drinks and decided to meet later that night.

Jimmy and Bertie were walking back to the estate when Bertie said to him, "Here, what about them Arabs ... they've got plenty of dough, ain't they, Jimmy?"

"Yeah, they have, but I was thinking more of robbing them, you know, get the girls to set them up and do the bastards. They carry a lot of dough around and they've always got gold on them. You know, chains, and Rolex watches, they all wear em.'

"Good thinking, Jimmy. What a brain."

Jimmy looked at Bertie and laughed. "Yeah, come on, I'm going home."

As Jimmy walked along his balcony, he knew that something was wrong. As soon as he got to his door, he noticed it was open just a fraction. He knew Mark wasn't back yet but his dad should have been in. Jimmy's hand slipped into his jeans pocket, feeling for the flick-knife. Jimmy pushed the door open with his foot and walked into his flat very slowly.

An arm grabbed him around the neck as he stepped into the living room. "What the fuck ..." is all he could say. The arm relaxed and he was pushed into the room. He tripped and fell against the fireplace. He looked around the room. His dad was sitting in his chair, a worried look on his face.

He mouthed, "Sorry, son." Over to his left, sitting in one of the dining chairs, was a small, smartly dressed, stocky man. He looked at Jimmy smiling. The arm that had grabbed him belonged to a big black guy, about 6ft 6in tall, weighing in at about 300lb.

"Help him up, Tommy," the man said to the black guy. "Help him up."

"I'll help myself, thanks," Jimmy said getting up. "Who the fuck are you and what are you doing in my house with that black bastard."

Tommy moved towards him. Jimmy taunted him. "Come on, motherfucker, I ain't scared of you, you fat bastard." Jimmy's hand went back into his pocket and gripped his flick-knife, ready for action if the black guy came near him.

"Leave him, Tommy, leave him." The small man got up and walked over to Jimmy. He smiled at him and said, "I've heard a lot about you, Jimmy Day. Big hero around here, got some nice little scams going. Blackmail, and trying to get into vice, not bad for a 17-year-old kid."

"I'm no fucking kid, mate. Anyway, who the fuck are you?"

"My name's Leo Stern and you, my lad, are stepping all over my manor and I don't like it. Rumour has it that you killed the Jamaican guy from Birmingham, but I shouldn't think you'd have the balls for that."

Jimmy looked at him saying nothing, just shrugged his shoulders.

"You're rubbing down one of my deals, the camera shop, Tottenham Court Road. Ring a bell, does it, Jimmy boy?" The man poked him in the stomach. "And it's got to stop, you hear? Let me tell you something, sonny. I control all vice, drugs, gambling – everything – in North London and you are getting in my way. You hear me? And it's going to fucking stop or I'll let me boy on you. You got that. Jimmy? From now on, what you make, I want half ... you got that, boy?" Leo looked at him, stony-faced.

Jimmy squared up to him, knowing that if he went for Leo, the big black guy would kill him. He had to have time to think this one out. There was no way he was giving anything to this little shit.

He looked at Leo and over to the black guy. "Look, you give me time ... I've got to tell the others, see what they say, know what I mean?"

"I don't know what you mean, just get it sorted and don't fuck me up, boy. You got any money on you now?" Leo asked.

Jimmy thought quickly. He put his hand into his inside pocket and took out one of the envelopes. "Here, I got this off a gay shopkeeper in St John's Wood. You take it."

Leo took the envelope and threw it at Tommy. "Count it," he said to him.

Tommy opened it and counted the money out. "Hundred quid, boss," Tommy said.

"Right, I'll be on my way. You keep that Tommy, give it to your missus. A present. Now show Jimmy Day how to respect me."

Before Jimmy could move, Tommy had punched him in the ribs twice. It felt like a hammer had hit him. He doubled over. Jimmy's dad jumped up and ran over to Leo. "You bastard, pick on someone your own size," he said.

"Fuck off, old man, you piss artist, or I'll break your fucking legs," the black guy said jumping in front of his boss.

"Right, Jimmy lad," Leo said to him, "hope you've got the message ... OK? Here," he threw a card on the carpet, "phone me when you're ready to pay me each week."

He looked at Jimmy's dad. "You've got balls, old man, for an old drunk. Come on, Tommy, let's be off … business calls." He looked again at Jimmy and smiled. "It's a man's world, boy, don't you forget it," and kicked him in the balls.

Whey they'd gone, Jimmy's dad helped him up. "What was that all about, son?" He looked bewildered. "Bloody hell."

Jimmy looked at his old man. "Thanks for helping me out, dad. It doesn't mean we're mates again yet, but I owe you one and don't worry about that piece of shit just gone out." His eyes smouldered with hatred. "I'll fucking have 'em both … I'll fucking have 'em, don't you worry."

Chapter 17

AT 8.30AM, JIMMY CLIMBED UP THE STAIRS TO BERTIE'S
FLAT ON THE FIFTH FLOOR. HE COULDN'T BE BOTHERED
TO WAIT FOR THE LIFT. IT WAS THE SAME AS JIMMY'S
PLACE – SAME COLOUR DOORS, SAME BALCONIES,
SAME EVERYTHING. NO WONDER PEOPLE WENT BARMY
IN COUNCIL FLATS.

He finally reached his mate's balcony. He walked up to
the door and knocked loudly. The door opened slowly. Mrs
Cooney stuck her head out and, seeing Jimmy, she opened
it wider.

"Hello, Jimmy boy, come in, come in," she said to him.

"Hi, Mrs Cooney ... Bertie in? Sorry I'm a bit early, but I
have to see him about a job someone wants doing."

Mrs Cooney didn't know about their criminal activities.

"Hope it pays well," she said "the Government should find

more jobs for youngsters, it's a shame, a damn shame. Want some breakfast, son?"

"Yes, please, Mrs Cooney ... bacon sarnie would do nice."

"Well, sit down and I'll wake up the boy ... "

Bertie came in ten minutes later, rubbing his eyes. "Blimey, Jimmy," he said, looking at his mate tucking into a bacon sarnie, "you're bloody early, something up?"

Bertie's mum came back into the kitchen carrying her coat and bag with her. "Right, I'm off. Bertie, your breakfast is over there on the oven, tea in the pot. See you tonight, I'm off to work." She looked at the wall clock, "I'm late already. Bye. Bye, Jimmy," and she was gone.

Bertie picked up his breakfast and walked over to the table where Jimmy was sitting. He sat down, looked at his mate and said between bites, "What's up, mate? You look all in. What time did you go to bed last night? You didn't come out with me ... you have a date or something?"

Jimmy finished off his sandwich, drank his tea, pushed his chair back and stretched his arms. "Not quite a date, more of an unplanned appointment, I would say," Jimmy said laughing.

"What you mean?" Bertie asked.

"Well, when I left you yesterday, about 5, wasn't it, I think? Anyway, when I got home, my door was open. Thinking my old man had left it open, but not quite sure, I edged in and ..."

Jimmy went on to tell him about everything that had happened, from Leo's threats from Leo to the kick in the balls when they left.

"Leo Stern came to your house to see you ... fucking hell, Jimmy. Don't you know who he is? And that bastard Tommy, he's a right killer. Stay clear of them, mate, stay clear, big fucking time."

"You know him?" Jimmy looked at his mate. "How do you know him?"

Bertie looked at him. "I don't know him. My dad told me about him, he's Mr Kingpin around North London. Bad news Jimmy, bad news. What did he want with you, then?" Bertie asked him.

"He wants me to lay off the scams I've been doing. The camera shop, that's his."

"Shit!" said Bertie.

"Yeah, big deal, but I ain't giving my scams up for that bastard. He said he'll give me until Friday to start giving him a cut of our profits. 50-50, he's got no chance."

"You're mad, Jimmy, he'll break our bleeding legs, you can bet your life on that," Bertie said to him. "How you going to get out of this one, mate?" Bertie looked deeply worried.

"I'll get something sorted, you wait and see. If I get the black guy sorted, Leo will be no problem, believe me. He, like most big-time boys, is all mouth. Get them by themselves and they don't want to know. See the bloke shot over the South last week ... pissed himself before they shot him, coward, know what I mean?

"Anyway, my old man tried to help me out so we're mates again at the moment. Oh, by the way, I'm going to Manchester Saturday to pick my brother up from my sister's house. You wanna come up with me?"

"What you going to sort out, mate?" Bertie asked. "They're big-time you know, its going to be tough."

"I've got an idea already, don't worry about it. If I show

133

fear, my whole gang will desert me. Talking of them, get 'em over The George tomorrow night. Get your girl over there, too, Bertie, I want her to do me a favour. Is she still in that clothes shop?"

"Yeah ... why, mate? You want her to nick some stuff for Sally or what?"

Jimmy looked at Bertie. "Just thought of something she can do for me ... and it ain't what you're thinking," he said laughing, pushing his mate on the shoulder. "Come on, get dressed ... I'm meeting Lenny down his yard at 11. He's getting something for me. By the way, Jackie's away on holiday, and so is Micky, both back next week. Gone down to Great Yarmouth with their parents."

It was just after 11.30am when they arrived at Lenny's yard at the back of the Caledonian Road. There was so much rubbish in there it was hard to spot Lenny who was always scruffy and dirty.

He was over in the corner of the yard taking the door off an old Ford. He looked up as they came over. "Hello, what you two want?" he said, and chuckled, "up to no good, I bet."

"Hi, Lenny," Jimmy said, "want you to get me something ... if you can that is."

"What's that, a sub-machine-gun?" he said grinning.

"No, nothing that noisy, Lenny. Listen, what I need is a needle, a knitting needle so sharp that it will go through a thick coat and into skin, and I also want a small bottle of acid."

"Fucking hell, Jimmy, who's upset you, mate?"

Jimmy told him everything that had happened to him the previous day. When he'd finished, he looked at Lenny and said, "Well, what would you do?"

"Same as you, mate. That Leo did a mate of mine a couple of years ago. Davy Lynch, you wouldn't know him, but Leo cut his thumb off."

"What for, Lenny?" Bertie asked.

"What for?" Lenny laughed. "He got behind in payments he owed him, which was only 200 quid. The bastard. When you want the stuff?"

"Don't know yet, Lenny, but I'll let you know when. Thanks."

They walked out of the yard towards the bus stop. Jimmy turned to Bertie. "Come on, mate, let's go down West. Have a burger and get some new gear, now I've settled that. Come on."

Chapter 18

**"BRING IN SERGEANT SANDERS, INSPECTOR, PLEASE,"
THE CHIEF INSPECTOR SAID TO ONE OF THE POLICEMEN
SAT NEXT TO HIM, "LET'S SEE WHAT HE'S GOT TO TELL
US ABOUT THIS SORRY AFFAIR."**

Sanders was at New Scotland Yard where an inquiry was being held about the death of young David Smith at West Central Police Station. He was there with his partner Detective John Rowley.

The Inspector got up from his chair, walked to the door, opened it, leaned out and shouted "Sergeant Ken Sanders, come in, please."

He walked back into the room followed by Sanders. The Inspector turned to Sanders and pointed to a chair in front of a desk where he addressed him formally.

"Sergeant Sanders, you have been asked to attend this

inquiry about David Smith who, at the time of his death, was in your custody." He introduced the two men beside him. "This is Chief Inspector Glenn, head investigator. To his left, Inspector Dors, his assistant.

"I am Inspector Miles ... I'm here to see that things go smoothly, like an umpire, if you like. We would like to ask you about the night in question."

Chief Inspector Glenn looked at him, trying to stare him out, and eventually spoke. "Sergeant, why do you think that this young lad took his own life? He was, according to ..." he picked up a sheet of paper and read " ... Inspector Cline of West Central, fine when he left you with the boy. He was perfectly all right, in fact. The Inspector told you that he was ready to let the boy go as soon as you had questioned him. Is that right?" he looked at the Sanders. "What went wrong?"

Sanders looked at the three officers in front of him. "You bastard," he thought to himself, "you're trying to badger me."

He looked at the Chief, then at the other two and said calmly, "Nothing went wrong as far as I was concerned. He was questioned just like anybody else, Sir. No shouting, bullying or anything else. We even gave him a cigarette, drink of Coke and something to eat. He was very calm, in fact."

Inspector Dors looked at Sanders, rubbed his chin and said, "Sergeant, did you touch the boy in any way, threaten him, make him think he was in big trouble? Think carefully, Sergeant ... was there anything you can remember which might have made him suicidal, sent him over the top? Did you shout at him at all?"

"No, Sir, I did none of those things and wouldn't anyway."

Inspector Miles stood up, walked around the desk and stood

behind Sanders. He spoke softly. "You know if there is any evidence that you caused the boy suffering during the investigation you, or your partner, will both be charged. You realise that, I hope. Anything, anything at all you want to tell us before you go?" he asked, walking back to his chair.

He sat down and looked at Sanders. "Well?"

"No, nothing at all, Sir," Sanders replied looking at the three of them in turn and said, "my conscience is clear, Sir."

Chief Inspector Glenn stood up and said to him, "You can go for now Sergeant, but you will be hearing from us shortly. Wait outside, please, and send your assistant in. Thank you."

As Sanders walked to the door, he opened it and was just about to go out when Inspector Miles called to him. "Oh, Sergeant, one last thing. Did young Smith cry at all when you were questioning him?"

Sergeant Sanders turned round and looked at the three investigators. Shrugging his shoulders, he said, "No, Sir, he didn't, why should he? He was too cocky to cry." He turned back to the open door and walked out.

Chief Inspector Glenn looked at his two officers when the room was empty and said, "Been in the force some years, Sergeant Sanders has. Been a good copper, his record is clean as a whistle. I hope for his sake and the police force he hasn't messed it up."

There was a knock at the door. "Come in, come in," the Chief said. The door opened and Detective John Rowley walked in.

"Ah, Rowley, sit down, man. Now, just want to ask you a few questions. You know what it's about, don't you?" Inspector Dors said to him.

"Yes, Sir," Rowley replied, not looking at all comfortable.

"Right then, tell me, when you and your Sergeant took over from Inspector Cline, what was David Smith like? I mean, what was his spirit like? Was he cocky, withdrawn, unhappy ... what?"

Detective Rowley looked at the Inspector, his hands fidgeting, a bead of sweat running off his nose and dropping on to his chin. He wiped it away with his hand, stretched his legs and shifted uneasily on the hard chair.

"He was all right, Sir, didn't seem at all nervous or frightened. A bit cocky, like most kids, but he answered most questions put to him. He looked a bit down when we last saw him but I put that down to tiredness, lack of sleep, I thought."

"Did Sergeant Sanders or yourself bully the lad into saying things he didn't want to say? Did you frighten him at all, in any way? You say he was in good spirits before you left, but then you say he looked a bit tired and a bit down in the mouth. Why? He thought he was going home. Inspector Cline told us he was happy and ready to go home before you and Sanders questioned him."

"I ... I ... I'm not sure, Sir, what happened. All I know is that he was OK when we questioned him and he was all right when we left him that night, Sir."

"Detective Rowley," Chief Glenn said to him, "if you are trying to protect anybody, don't, because you will be in serious trouble, my lad, serious trouble. You hear me?"

"Yes, Sir, and I'm not trying to protect anyone."

"Off you go, Detective, and send in WPC Shaw, would you, please?"

As he got up to go, Inspector Miles once again asked,

"Rowley, did David Smith cry a lot or just a little?"

"Just a little, Sir,", then realising what he had said, he added "not that I noticed anyway."

He walked out of the room and closed the door. Inspector Dors turned to Chief Glenn and said, "If them two didn't cause that boy's death then I'm a bloody Dutchman," and he banged the table in anger.

The Chief looked at him. "I know how you feel, Larry, but without evidence our hands are tied."

The door opened slowly and WPC Shaw poked her head around the door. "Sir?" she said, "can I come in?"

"Yes, certainly. Come in, Shaw. Sit down," the Chief said.

After he explained to her what was happening and who was who, Inspector Dors opened the questioning.

"Now, WPC Shaw, only a few questions for you," he said, trying to put her ease. "On the night in question, you were in the interview room and on the desk when this tragic event happened. Is that correct?"

"Yes, Inspector," she said, looking at him in the eye.

Dors looked at her as if trying to read her mind. "Did Inspector Cline do or say anything to David Smith that would upset the lad? You know. grab hold of him or threaten him in any way?"

"No, Sir," Shaw said, "he was quite the opposite, very gentle with him. Didn't force him to do anything or say anything he didn't want to, Sir."

Inspector Miles cut in. "What about Sergeant Sanders and Detective Rowley. Did they say anything to you about what went on in the interview room that night?"

"No, nothing, Sir, why should they? It was nothing to do

with me after Inspector Cline had finished with the young lad, Sir."

"Quite, Shaw, quite. When the constable found the body, were you there?"

"No, Sir, I was making a cup of tea in the canteen at the time, Sir."

"WPC Shaw," Chief Glenn took over, "when you were outside the room on duty at the desk, did you hear any noise or crying coming from the interview room when the boy was being questioned by Sergeant Sanders and Detective Rowley." He looked at her with a pleading look in his eyes. "Think clearly, Shaw, anything at all?"

The policewoman looked at the three officers in front of her. She leant back in her chair, sighed and said to them, "I heard loud shouting coming from the room, Sir, and later very loud sobbing. I knew it was David Smith, but couldn't do anything because..."

"Because you were scared, Shaw, is that it?"

"Yes, Sir," she said.

Chief Glenn looked at her sensing that she was about to cry. He said kindly, "Do you think Sergeant Sanders and Detective Rowley went too far with young Smith? I mean, were they too aggressive with him, which could have led to him taking his own life?"

WPC Shaw looked at them, tears starting to tumble down her cheeks. Nodding her head, and trying to wipe the tears away from her eyes with the back of her hand, she replied, "Yes, I do, Sir. I think they bullied him into submission until his mind went, the poor boy."

"Thank you, Shaw, you may go now. You may hear from us

in the near future," Inspector Miles said to her. "Here," he handed her a handkerchief, "use this to dry your eyes."

When she had gone, Chief Glenn said to the other two investigators, "Brave girl ... brave girl. I wish we had more like her in the force. I've already got Inspector Cline's view and the constable on duty that night. I think we might have enough here on the Sergeant and his partner. What do you think, Larry?" he said, addressing Inspector Dors.

"I think we might have them, Chief. Let's see what the Public Prosecutor has to say, shall we?"

Chapter 19

"DID YOU SEE THAT CHIEF INSPECTOR'S BLOODY FACE? HE WAS LOVING EVERY MINUTE OF THAT INVESTIGATION," SERGEANT SANDERS SAID TO DETECTIVE ROWLEY AS THEY WERE DRIVING BACK TO THEIR OWN POLICE STATION IN KING'S CROSS.

The Chief Inspector had let them go, saying they would hear from him if anything came from the investigation.

"He wants to blame us for Smith's death, Sarge," Rowley said, keeping his eyes on the road. They were stuck in a traffic jam in Whitehall. "Bloody traffic."

"Use your bloody blue light, man, let's get out of this sodding jam," Sanders said. "I've got a lot of bloody work to do today and I don't need this as well."

"I thought you were taking your missus out tonight, Sarge, for a meal, you said. Ain't it her birthday or something?"

"It can wait. Theres's always Christmas," Sanders said, looking at his watch. It was just after 7. Monday nights were always the worst, he thought to himself. "Come on, John, get that bloody siren going."

They reached the station just after 7.30pm.

"Right, Detective," Sanders said, "get that file on that gang fight, will you? There must be something in there to help us out somewhere."

"Right, Sarge," Rowley said as he walked out of their office and into the larger room at the back of the station where all the files were kept on local criminal activity.

* * *

Linda James was walking up Kentish Town Road with her best mate Sheila Higgs, known affectionately by the gang as 'The Slapper'. It was Sunday night and Linda was saying to her mate, "I'll have that bastard, you know, Sheila. He let all them bastards rape me that night. I'll get something on Jimmy fucking Day, you'll see."

"You told your ma yet, Lin?" Sheila asked her, chewing gum and trying to blow a bubble.

"Not bloody likely ... my mum thinks the sun shines out of Jimmy's arse. There's no way she'd believe me. I wouldn't waste my time telling her anyway, no chance."

"Why don't you let it go, Linda? Don't forget, you were pissed that night so you really can't remember all that happened. That's what you told me, didn't you?"

"You've got to be kidding, Sheila, I'm not letting him off the hook that easy. I'll get him one way or the other."

Sheila laughed. "Knowing you, Linda, it will be the other," she said and carried on giggling.

Linda pushed her, nearly knocking her over. "Cheeky cow," she said laughing. "Come on, let's go up The George, see if anybody's in there. Feel like a good drink."

"Yeah, and you're only 16," Sheila laughed again. "Jimmy and the boys might be in there."

"Who cares? Fuck him and the rest of them," Linda said.

Sheila burst into fits of laughter again. "You already have, Linda."

They both roared with laughter and walked on up the High Street.

* * *

Jimmy was leaning on his mate Bertie's shoulder. The entire gang were sitting on the wall in the vast estate. Pete Higgins was talking and was lighting a cigarette at the same time. "You found anything out about Dave Smith, Jimmy?" he asked looking at his hero.

"Na, nothing yet, but one of Jackie's mum's mates works in West End Central nick. She does early morning cleaning and Jackie's dad has told her to keep her eyes and ears open, ain't she, Jackie?" Jimmy said, looking at Jackie Todd.

"That's right, mate. My mum will find out something ... she's a nosy old cow when she wants to be."

Micky spoke up as Jackie finished talking. "You know old Benji, the tramp who hangs about the estate, Jimmy?"

"Yeah, what's he got the fuck to do with this conversation and what does an old tramp know that we don't? Tell me!"

"Well, let me finish, Jimmy. The night Dave topped himself, he ..."

"Hang on, hang on," Paul White shouted out. "We don't know he hung himself yet."

"All right, all right" Micky said, "we don't know. Anyway, Benji, the tramp, was in the cells that night, got arrested for being supposedly drunk and disorderly, but he was just pretending so he could get a bed for the night."

"Fucking get on with it, Micky, I want a drink tonight," Bertie moaned.

"Well, when I was talking to him this morning, he told me that him and his mate heard very loud crying and it was about the same time that the Scottish bastard and his mate were there questioning Dave."

"Are you serious? Don't mess me about, Micky," Jimmy said, anger flashing in his blue eyes. "If that bastard caused Dave's death, I'll kill him, even if it takes me a lifetime."

"What's the time?" He looked at his watch. "It's just after 9. Come on, last in the pub buys."

* * *

Detective Rowley was sat in Sergeant Sanders' office, his feet up on the desk. He was reading a file report on the gang fight weeks ago between the Asians and the Camden boys, which culminated in the Asian kid, Beddal Mistry who lost his hand. The kid refused to tell the police who'd chopped his hand off. He didn't know why the white boys had attacked them in the first place.

"I bet you didn't," Rowley said out loud to himself as he

flipped through the pages of the file. He came to another report by the officer who was sent to investigate the incident. It read: "Of all the Asian boys interviewed, not one of them would volunteer any information, even the boy who lost his hand or the young girl whose arm was broken. They wouldn't say anything at all about the white boys, only that they'd sort their own thing out."

Rowley stopped reading and put the file down. "Sanders has got more chance of kissing the Queen than catching Jimmy Day and his gang over this," Rowley said to himself, taking his feet off the desk and standing up.

He stretched his arms above his head and looked at the big wall clock. The phone rang. He picked it up and said, "Rowley here, CID. Can I help you?"

"Hello, John, it's me, Ken. Did you read the file?"

"Yeah, Sarge." He sat down again, opening up the file. "Not a bloody sausage. We can't get anything on Dave, I'm afraid. Not a thing on the gangfight either. There's nothing in this file that would convict anyone at all, Sarge."

"Bloody hell, I don't believe it" Sanders bellowed down the phone. He went quiet, then said, "What about the black guy found in the arches? Anything there at all?"

"Yeah, he was traced. His name was Olu Mabumba. Came from Nigeria originally, lived in Birmingham. Heavily into drug dealing, wanted in Holland on a rape charge. Birmingham and Manchester police wanted him for selling drugs to kids, Sarge."

"Good fucking riddance. Whoever did him deserves a medal."

"I thought you were at the theatre with your missus, Sarge,"

Rowley said, looking at the clock. It was just after 10.30pm.

"I am, I am. We've just come out. Going for a meal. Look, I'll see you tomorrow. You on until 4?"

"Yeah, Sarge. I'm just going for my supper down the canteen. Have a good time. See you. Goodnight," Rowley said and put the phone down.

Chapter 20

BEDDAL MISTRY WAS SITTING IN THE BACK OF HIS FATHER'S SHOP. AT THE END OF HIS RIGHT ARM WHERE HIS HAND USED TO BE WAS A BANDAGED STUMP. HE WAS HOLDING IT UP TO SHOW HIS FRIEND RASHID SITTING NEXT TO HIM.

"What you going to do about that boy, Jimmy Day?" his friend said to him, pointing to his stump. "You letting him get away with that?"

Beddal frowned at him, anger showing in his dark eyes.

"No, I'm not. Look at me. I'm bloody 17 years old with no right hand. I'll get him soon. Next week, my cousins and their friends are coming over for a wedding. They are all staying overnight, Friday, before the wedding. That's the night we'll strike. There will be about 60 of us. I know his haunts, where he'll be. We'll get them all as they come out of the pub. I must

151

have revenge for this, even though my mother tries to talk me out of it. My father, he won't talk to me. 'It will affect my business, forget it,' he said. As if it will go away and my hand will reappear. God, I'm so angry with him, he's turning more English every day. All he thinks about is his shop."

Rashid looked at him. "I feel for you, mate ... can't wait until Friday. We'll show them white boys the Asian way to fight."

"No, no, I just want Jimmy Day. I will do to him as he has done to me. We've got to get him away from his mates. They'll fight to the death for him, believe me, but take him away from them and he's hopeless."

"Yeah ... how we going to do that?" Rashid asked, not looking too hopeful.

Beddal looked at him and said, "Look, mate, wait till next week and I'll show you, OK?"

"All right. Has that copper been around again?" Rashid asked.

"He's round every other day. I keep telling him no way I'll say anything. The copper says I'll end up in trouble, not them. Tell me a name, he says, and he won't bother you again. Bloody cops, they think it's so easy."

Beddal's father came into the back of the shop. Seeing his son talking to his mate, he put two and two together and said, "You bring shame to my house ... you find another home," and walked out.

* * *

Detective Rowley was walking along Hampstead Road with

152

his partner, Ken Sanders. It was Monday morning, bright and breezy for September.

Looking at Sanders, he said, "It's 10.30, Sarge. How about going round Jimmy Day's place? It's only across the way and you can bet your life he'll be in."

Sanders looked at him. "You know, John, that's a bloody good idea. Come on."

Once they'd arrived at the flat, Rowley knocked on the door, not seeing the bell to his left.

"Knock louder, man, knock louder," Sanders said, irritated.

Finally, the door opened and a head appeared. "Yes, what do you want?"

"Jimmy Day in?" Sanders asked, showing his badge. "Want to ask him a few questions. Can you get him for me, son?"

Mark looked at him, half-asleep, and said through a yawn, "He's in ..."

"Who's that, Mark?" a voice came from behind the door, which was opening wider. Jimmy Day stood there in his shorts looking half-dead. He peered through half-shut eyes.

"What do you want?" he asked seeing the coppers. "Ain't you got no cars to stop for bad tyres or something?"

Sanders fixed him with a glare. "Don't be bloody cheeky, boy ... I want to ask you a few questions. Won't take long, boy." He stepped over the doorstep and into the hallway.

"Here, fucking get out," Jimmy said to him, "you can't do that."

"Well, I've done it, and if you don't like it, I'll get a warrant to get you in. What do you say to that, boy?"

"Stop calling me 'boy', copper ... and what do you want?" He looked round at his brother. "Mark, get to your room until I call you."

"Right, Jimmy. You want me to fetch Dad? He's only next door," Mark asked him.

"No thanks, Mark. Go on, get going."
When he had gone, Jimmy turned to the coppers. "Well?"

"Look, Day, I know and you know that you hacked that Asian kid's hand off. The whole fucking neighbourhood knows and I'll tell you this ... " Sanders took a step toward Jimmy, "I'm going to get you for it, you little bastard."

Rowley stepped in front of his Sergeant and said, "Let me at him, Sarge, the cheeky bastard."

"Na, leave him," Sanders said, putting his hand out to stop Rowley from doing anything silly. "That's what he wants. Come on, someone will grass him up."

He looked at Jimmy, whose eyes were blazing. "Don't worry, lad, I'll be back. I'll get you ... There will be someone out there who wants you nicked and that day will come, believe me, laddie. Let's go Detective."

They walked out of the door, on to the landing. Sanders looked around at Jimmy still standing in the doorway, a big grin on his face.

"You can smile now, Day, but I'll wipe that grin off your face, don't worry," and he walked off with his partner.

As Sanders and Rowley came out of the lift on the ground floor and into the yard, they both looked up at the flats. They could see Jimmy leaning over his balcony.

"I'll fucking have him, Detective. I'll have him ..." Sanders said. "Come on back to the nick. I want you to look through anything on his gang. One of them must have a weak spot and I'll bloody find it."

Mark came out of his bedroom, walked through the flat and on to the balcony where his brother stood.

"What was that about, Jimmy ... them cops got you on something?" he asked, looking worried.

"Na, they said they were looking for someone and, as I mostly know everyone around here, they thought I might be able to help them. Some fucking chance."

"Oh, that's OK then ... you want some breakfast, Jimmy?"

"No thanks. Just a cuppa, I've got to ring Bertie."

He walked back into the flat and into the living room, picked up the phone and started dialling.

"Hi, Bertie, it's me, Jimmy. You going round picking the money up today?" He paused for the reply. "Well, take Micky and Jackie with you."

"What?"

"Yeah, just them two ... and listen, you've got ten places to go to. Just over a 1,000 quid. Bring it over tonight, I'll be in about 6 and, by the way, Mark says thanks for going with me to Manchester to pick him up. He enjoyed the trip and thanks from me, too."

"What, yeah, it is a dump up there, they've only just got TV. You can keep Manchester. What a hick place. Right, see you later."

Jimmy looked at his watch, it was nearly midday. "Got to go, see you, Bertie," and he put the phone down. "Mark, you dressed yet?" he shouted to his brother. "I've got the DSS coming round soon."

His brother walked into the living room still in his pyjamas and said, "No, not yet, why?"

"Well, don't wear anything good. Wear all your old gear,

155

look scruffy. I will, it's the only way to get more money off them bastards."

"Right, Jimmy, I'll do that now."

Jimmy got up, looked in the pantry and took out a big cardboard box. He walked back into the living room, looked around, walked over to the old sideboard, and opened it up. He took all the bottles of spirits out until only a bottle of lemonade was left. He put them all into the box, picked it up and walked into the kitchen.

Putting the box down on the table, he then walked over to the fridge-freezer and opened it up. It was crammed full of food. He opened the bottom half, which contained the cold box. It, too, was full of steaks, frozen pizzas, chickens, bacon. Jimmy laughed to himself and said out loud, "Blimey, if that old fart from the DSS see's this lot, she'll have twins."

He quickly emptied both compartments, leaving just a little food in each. He knew that sometimes they looked all round the flat and always in the fridge-freezer.

"Fuck 'em," he said. "Mark, you ready yet?"

"Yeah, Jimmy," Mark said as he came into the room. Jimmy laughed; his brother looked like one of the orphan boys from Oliver.

"What you think, bruv?" Mark asked. "Will I pass?"

"You'll do," Jimmy said. He looked at his watch again. "Come on, let's get this stuff next door and get the old man in here."

In ten minutes, they were back in their own flat with their dad. They were just in time; there was a knock at the door.

Jimmy laughed. "That bloody bell never gets rung. I'll have to raise it a bit. Go and answer the door, Mark."

When the lady from the DSS had had a good look round and had spoken to Jimmy's dad for a while, she said, "Well, Mr Day, we're going to give you an extra £10 a week. It will help you out a bit more and I'll give you an allowance for clothes for the boys, but I want to see the receipts, OK?" she said looking at Jimmy and Mark.

"Can't you get a job yet, Jimmy," she asked. "Big lad like you, you're 17 now and the money we're giving your dad won't be coming in for ever."

"He's really trying, Mrs Miller," Jimmy's dad said to her. "A lot of the sites won't take him on as he's too young. Safety and all that," he said. "Ain't that right, son?"

"That's right, Dad … not interested in the young any more. They want cheap labour from abroad. Asians and all them lot."

"Now, now Jimmy," she said, handing over a cheque to Jimmy's dad. "Here, Mr Day, there's £100 for some new clothes for the boys and you'll get your extra allowance money on Friday. Send the receipts to me at the office."

She got up and walked over to the fridge-freezer, opened the door, closed it and looked around at the three of them.

"Oh dear … you must buy more food. That boy is as skinny as a rake."

After she had gone, they had a good laugh. Jimmy looked at Mark. "You ought to eat more, my boy, you look as skinny as a rake."

"Yeah, and you should buy some nice clothes, dear boy, you look like a tramp."

They all started to snigger again, Jimmy collapsing on his chair in fits of laughter.

* * *

The rain pelted down on Jimmy and his mates as the walked down Shaftesbury Avenue, each of them chewing burgers.

"Cor, Jimmy, can't we get out of this bloody rain?" Paul White said, looking at his leader. "My burger's bloody saturated." He threw it on the pavement in disgust.

"Shut up, Gummy, I'm thinking," Jimmy glared at him, the rain dripping off his baseball cap and down on to his nose, making him sneeze.

"Bless you, mate," Bertie said to him. He patted him on the back. "How about taking in a movie, it'll keep us dry at least?"

"Yeah, how about it, Jimmy?" Sammy shouted to him, "I'm bloody freezing and feel like a drowned rat."

Bertie looked at him, laughing, "You look like a bloody rat, mate."

They turned into Great Windmill Street, near Piccadilly Circus, a side street full of sandwich bars and strip joints. Some of the girls were sitting on the doorsteps. As they came nearer, one of the girls stood up and spoke to Jimmy. "Want a good time, dearie? Won't cost you lot. I'll take the lot of you for 100 – cash."

Jimmy looked at her, smiled and spoke softly, "I wouldn't give you 50 pence, you old slapper. Fuck off!"

She looked at him with contempt. "You better piss off, boy, or I'll have my man on you, cheeky sod."

Jimmy grabbed her hand, twisting it until she cried out. He spoke to her again. "You send who you bloody like, darling," he pulled her to him, her breath coming in heavy gasps, "I'll cut his bloody heart out." He let go of her, she stumbled back into the doorway and disappeared, the darkened hall swallowing her up.

"Come on you, lot, let's go in there," Jimmy said, pointing to the old Windmill Theatre across the way, which was lit up with neon lights; 'Line Dancing'. All Welcome! YOUNG and OLD.

"You have got to be kidding," Bertie said, "I ain't bloody going in there, it's like Irish dancing, that's for the girls, mate.

"Yeah, you're right, Bertie," Sammy said, 'It's a poof's dance as well."

"Not for me, mate, either," Paul said, "Come on, Jimmy, I ask ya!"

Jimmy looked at each of them in turn, saying, "Look, it's only 'til the rain eases off ... what you say?"

They looked at him and then at each other. Bertie spoke up. "As long as we don't have to do that bloody dance, right, boys?"

"Right," they all said together.

They walked across the road and into the big foyer of the theatre. A woman dressed in cowboy gear came across to them.

"Hello, boys. Come in, come in – go right in, the band are just doing a warm up.

"Thanks, love," Jimmy said to her. "Come on, boys." They walked past her after paying the £2 entrance fee.

"It's cheaper than the movies, anyway," Paul said. "It might be quite a laugh."

They walked through the big swing bat-wing doors into the big hall, which had been made to look like a saloon bar.

"Cool, Jimmy, look at all them lovely birds – wow," Bertie said.

Another woman came over to them, a pretty blonde, also dressed in cowboy gear. She smiled at them. Taking hold of Jimmy's arm, she said, "Sit over there and you can see how it's done. You ever done it before?" She looked at Micky as they sat down.

"Yeah, every Saturday night, darling," Micky said. He laughed.

"Shut up," Jimmy glared at him. He spoke to the blonde woman. "Take no notice of him, miss."

"That's OK," she said, and walked away blushing.

Half-an-hour had gone by and the place had filled up. People were dancing, talking and milling around. One of the girls walked on to the stage, a microphone in her hand. "Right, everyone, we want some volunteers to come up here and do a dance. We don't care how you dance or what style. It's just a bit of fun we have every week ... come on then. Come on. Who's it going to be?"

The pretty blonde woman came over to Jimmy and the boys. "Come on, boys, I'm sure you can dance, come and have a go?" she pleaded.

Jimmy looked at her, then at the boys, who were pretending not to hear. He smiled, paused and then said, "OK, love, we'll do it."

"No way, Jimmy," Paul shouted.

"On yer bike, mate," Micky said.

"Not a chance in hell," said Bertie, looking at Jimmy. "You're the only dancer here. You do it."

Jimmy looked at the blonde again and said, "OK, Calamity Jane, that means they will do it. Come on, boys, let's go!"

They all trooped up on the stage, moaning at Jimmy. The crowd in the hall clapped and whistled at them, some of them shouting, "Come on, boys, show us a leg" and "get 'em off!"

The boys weren't happy. "Let's fuck off, Jimmy."

"Shut up," Jimmy said to them. "Let's have a bloody laugh for a change. Put some music on, sweatheart, I'll show you how it's done."

They all stood in line as as the woman put a record on. It was "Blanket on the Ground" by Billie Jo Spears, a very catchy tune. After a couple of seconds, the boys started to get the beat; they swayed, sashayed and stomped. The crowd were going mad, especially the young girls.

When the music finished, they jumped off the stage to rapturous applause.

"That was great, boys," the blonde woman said to them. "You sure can dance!"

"Think nothing of it, darling!" Micky said proudly, "it was nothing."

"Oh, shut up, Micky. Come on, boys, let's move, it's getting late, and we're out tonight," Jimmy said. He looked across at the woman. "Thanks for having us ... see you again, maybe." He looked at his gang. "Let's move it!"

The woman watched them walk out of the theatre, thinking to herself, "Funny bunch, but great dancers."

Chapter 21

MOST OF THE GANG WERE LOUNGING ON BERTIE'S LIVING ROOM FLOOR. IT WAS MONDAY NIGHT, HIS PARENTS WERE AT BINGO.

"Not likely to win," Bertie said to the rest of them as they attacked his dad's beer and whisky. "I don't think my mum's won since she came over from the old country," he added.

"You get your visit from the DSS, Jimmy?" Paul asked, trying to eat a mouthful of fish and chips which Micky had brought in for them all. "Eat and enjoy," he had said to them.

"Yeah, old Mrs Miller was round this morning. She's OK. Anyway, she gave my dad more money and the old man conned her out of 100 quid for new clothes for us," Jimmy laughed.

"Its so easy to get money ... no wonder these illegal immigrants come over by the shipload. Anyway, Bertie, how'd you get on this morning, any trouble?"

163

Bertie stood up, stuck his hand in his pocket and brought out a wad of money.

"Here you go, mate, only 120 short. The dry cleaner's shop wasn't open. Gone over to see his parents in Turkey. Left a note in his window."

Jimmy took the money from his mate. "Thanks, Bertie … share it out with the boys." He gave the bundle back to Bertie. "And put that money the Turk owes us in the book, that'll be 300 he owes."

"Right, mate." Bertie took the money and started to split it between everyone.

"Oh, Bertie," Jimmy said, "give Dave's dad 100, he's still part of us, if you know what I mean."

"Sure, Jimmy," Bertie said, "great idea."

"Nice one, Jimmy," Micky chipped in. "We're with you, Jimmy," Jackie Todd shouted.

"Nice one, mate," said Sammy after he let out an almighty fart.

"Do you have to, Sammy?" Bertie said, giving him his share of the money, "you smell like a skunk."

"It must be them chips. I feel a fart coming on," Paul said, bursting out laughing.

"Anyway, lads, when you have all finished, there's a rumour going round that the Asians are looking for a rematch with us and it looks like its going to be a big one. My informant tells me that there's going to be a big Paki wedding in a couple of weeks or so, and the one who lost his hand will be at the wedding with his cousins and clan, so it could be that weekend the fight might go down."

Paul White stood up and said to them, "It should have been

his fucking head." He was guffawed while trying to drink a can of beer and eat chips at the same time.

"All right, all right," Jimmy said, "now until I get more information on them Pakis, there's not a lot we can do. They hardly ever come over to our manor so we can't have a go at them again yet. Let them come to us, it's better to fight on our own turf. I ain't too bothered what they do anyway."

"Who's giving you all the info, Jimmy?" Sammy asked him. "Can you trust him?"

"It's a her actually. A girl who works in the mini-market told me. She works part-time at weekends. Said she heard two of the Asians talking in the back of the shop but someone came in and she didn't hear everything."

"That's Paula Young. I used to go out with her last year," Micky Taret said, "a right little raver, that one. Her dad's inside doing five years for shooting some geezer who was supposed to have grassed him up. Comes out next year. I was talking to her last week … she's OK."

"I know … that's why she told me, dickhead," Jimmy snarled at Micky.

"What we going to do if they come at us all of a sudden, Jimmy?" Bertie asked. "We won't even know the day they're gonna come at us."

"We will, I promise you. I'll know in advance, believe me, and I promise you this … it will be more than a bloody hand missing when I get hold of that fucking Asian again."

* * *

Sergeant Sanders sat at his desk. He had been flipping

through the files of the gang fight for two hours but couldn't find a thing that pointed to Jimmy Day.

"I bloody know it was you, you little bastard!" he muttered to himself.

"What was that Sarge?" Rowley said, coming into the room with two coffees balanced in one hand. He kicked the door shut with his foot. "You talking to yourself again," he laughed.

"No, not really, just trying to get that bloody gang fight cleared up, but all I've got here is events, happenings, but no names … and without names I can't do a bloody thing. Even the Asians ain't saying nothing. You know what that means, John, don't you?"

"No, Sarge, not really. What?" Rowley asked with a "I don't know what the hell you're talking about" look on his face.

"It means that there is going to be another big gang fight, doesn't it?"

"Of course. Yeah, yeah, you could be right, and by the look on your face, Sarge, this could be what we've been waiting for. Am I right?"

"You've hit the nail on the head, laddie, that's it. Now all we have to do is find out where and when it will be. And how are we going to find out? You got any snitches around Camden any more, John?"

"One … well, used to have, but ain't seen him for quite a while," Rowley said.

"Well, get hold of him if you can, see if he can find out anything at all. If there's going to be a gang fight or whatever. If your snitch can get us that information, I've got Day, 'cause he will more or less do the same thing as before, or worse, you can bet your life on that."

Rowley looked at Sanders and said, "Look Sarge, I know that Day kid is only 17 but he's got the mind of an adult. He's no mug, believe me. He'll know that you will be sniffing around."

"Just get your snitch working on it, John, all right?" Sanders said to him. He shut the files and stood up. He looked at his watch, it was just after 9.30pm.

"Stick them files away for me, laddie. I don't think we'll need them for a while."

* * *

Young Mark Day was queuing up for fish and chips with his dad, around the corner from the estate where they lived.

"Where's Jimmy tonight, Mark?" his dad asked.

"He's round Bertie's, I think, Dad. Why?"

"Na, nothing son … you never know with your brother. I do like to know what he's doing, you know."

Mr Day had heard around the estate that his son was immersing himself deeper and deeper into his own private world. "He thinks he's Al Capone," his drinking buddy Henry had told him down at his local pub. "He'll be in big, big trouble, mate, if he don't watch it. You let him have his own way too much."

"He won't do anything I tell him any more. He goes his own way but he's good to me. We've only just started talking. First time for years," Mr Day confided.

"I heard you had a visit from our local gangster, Leo, and his minder the other week. Watch them, mate, he'll have your guts for garters," Henry said.

"Yeah, Leo Stern, the short-arse. It's his minder you've got to watch. I went for him but he threw his arms up. Look at me, no bloody chance," Day said.

"Dad, dad, what you want?" Mark was tugging at his arm.

"Oh, sorry, son, miles away." He gave his order, they waited, got their supper and went home.

As they walked into the estate, Mark nudged his dad and said, "There, look, Dad, there's a load of Pakis over there on the grass bank. What they want?"

"Just walk on by, lad, ignore them. It looks like they're waiting for someone and I don't think it's us. Come on."

As they walked to the entrance of their block of flats, one of the Asians came up to them.

"You're Jimmy Day's dad, ain't you?" he said to Mr Day.

"Yeah, what's it to you? And what you doing on this estate, boy. Your taking a chance …"

"Maybe I am, but tell your son Jimmy, I'm coming to see him soon. Very soon. You remember that, old man." Without turning back, he walked out of the estate with his mates.

"What was that all about, Dad" Mark said to his dad.

Mr Day looked at his young son. "Nothing to worry about, son, nothing that Jimmy can't handle I hope. Come on, the supper's getting cold."

Chapter 22

"HEY, MATE, THE PHONE'S RINGING," JIMMY SAID PUNCHING BERTIE ON THE ARM. "ITS MOST PROBABLY YOUR BIRD, SHE'S GOT YOU CORNERED, MATE," HE SAID LAUGHING.

"Yeah, she wishes," Bertie replied, jumping up and walking over to the phone. He turned round before he picked it up, saying to the others, "Shut it, boys, keep it down a minute."

He picked the phone up. "Yeah, who is it?" He bellowed into the phone. "Yeah, he is why …? Hang on," he looked at Jimmy. "Its Morris Wright, he wants you, mate," he said as he handed the phone over.

"What you want Morris?" Jimmy asked, trying to drink a whisky while speaking. "When was that. They fucking what? Right, we're on our way."

He slammed the phone down and looked at his gang. "Right, let's move, them fucking Asians have been in our estate. Morris saw them talking to my old man and Mark. I'll fucking kill that Asian bastard this time. Come on, let's see if they're still around."

"Need any weapons, Jimmy?" Pete Higgins asked him, punching his fist into his other hand. "Let's fucking cut 'em up good this time."

"Not this time, Looney, they'll be gone by now. Anyway, I've got to go and see what they said to Mark and the old man. Let's go."

The estate was deathly quiet as Jimmy and his gang walked into the big courtyard below the flats. They moved over to the grass bank where Morris Wright said he'd seen and heard the Asian gang.

"Nothing there, Jimmy," Micky Taret said running back to them after he'd looked around the back of the flats. "Its so quiet, not a dickie bird, they've long gone, mate. What's to do?"

Jimmy looked at his gang. "Look, you all go home. Micky's right, they've long gone. Its after 10 anyway, I'll see you all tomorrow. Come on, let's go."

Jimmy walked along his balcony swearing to himself. "The shit," he kept muttering, "I'll fucking kill him."

He put the key in the lock of the front door, turned it and pushed the door open. He walked into the hallway, took his long coat off and his cap, hung them up on the pegs on the wall and walked into the living room.

His dad was sitting in the armchair watching the telly. "Watcha boy you're early, ain't ya, all your mates gone home?"

Jimmy looked at his dad, even though he didn't like him much, he had to keep the peace mostly because of his brother.

"Yeah, I was told them bleeding Asians were bothering you and Mark that's why I'm home early. What they say to you?" Jimmy walked over to the settee and sat down. "They threaten you at all? Was Mark scared? Them bastards!"

His dad looked at him, shaking his head. "No, the Asian lad was quite polite. Funny … too polite, if you get my drift. No, they didn't threaten us. There was only two of them, told me to tell you that he'll see you very soon, then they walked off. You're in deep, Jimmy. That lad had only one hand. It was you and your lot who did that to him, wasn't it?"

"Yeah, and who gives a fuck? Nobody! I did it all right and I'll do it again, you wait and see."

"You're crazy, son … the Old Bill will get you, you can bet your life on that. They're most probably watching you now."

"Look, Dad, I can look after myself and I know that Scottish bastard copper is watching me but I'll never let them bastards take me and do to me what they did to Dave, no fucking chance."

Jimmy leaned back on the settee, yawned and stood up. He looked at his dad again and said, "Look, Dad, I know we've had our differences in the past. Let's put them aside for a while, all right. See you in the morning. Goodnight."

His dad sat there thinking about what his elder son had said to him. "He might listen to me … and, then again, he might bloody not."

Day walked over to the cabinet in the corner and took out a bottle of beer. He opened it up, lit a cigarette, went into the hallway and opened the front door. He walked out on to the balcony, took a sip of beer, then a drag on his cigarette and said out loud, "What a fucking life."

* * *

Bedel Mistry looked at his mate Rashid. "Well, what?" he said.

His friend looked at him, shaking his head. "You shouldn't have gone over to that estate tonight, mate … you've let Jimmy Day know that we're going after him. I can't believe you did that."

"I know, I know, it was a stupid mistake but I was so angry that I had to get it out of my system," Bedel said, "but don't worry … neither he nor his gang know when we're going to hit them."

He stood up, walked over to his mate, slapped him on the shoulder and said "Revenge is mine, sayeth the Lord. Time to go home, mate, its after midnight." He carried on talking as he walked to the door with his friend.

"You're still at school, I'm not any more. Get plenty of sleep, my friend, I'll see you later."

* * *

Linda James was lying on the settee in her living room. Lying next to her was Morris Wright. They had just had a shag. Morris sat up, and zipped up his jeans. "Cor, that was great, Linda … thought you didn't like me. Why the sudden change?"

Linda looked at him, smiling "Well, Morris, you know everyone know's I'm Jimmy's girl, and if he finds out that you've been screwing me, you're dead. You know that, Morris don't you?"

Morris looked at her, fear written all over his face. "You ain't going to tell him, Linda, are you? I thought you two didn't get on any more?"

"No, we're still seeing each other," she lied, "in fact, I was supposed to see him tonight, but I told him I was washing my hair."

"So why did you invite me round, and why let me screw you if you're Jimmy's girl? Bloody hell, I've only just phoned him about them fucking Asians and I'm in your house using your bloody phone. God! He could find out I've been here. Please don't tell him."

The fear in his eyes made Linda laugh. "Don't worry, Morris, I ain't going to tell him."

She got up, pulling up her knickers and brushing her skirt down. "Look at your spunk all over my mum's settee. She'll do her nut. I'll have to clean that up before I go to bed."

"Don't worry, Linda, your mum will think it's one of her lovers."

She glared at him. "Don't be so fucking cheeky, you arsehole," she said to him punching him on the arm, "and I invited you round here because I know you fancied me ... and I need a favour as well."

"Yeah, and what's that?" Morris sneered at her.

"Just let me know when Jimmy's going to do that Leo Stern. You know that gangster he's having trouble with?"

"He won't tell me, Linda, I'm not in his gang. I just give him info about things now and then, that's all."

She looked at him, walking over. She started to rub his cock inside his jeans with her hand. "You get information for me and you can have me all you want," she said, kissing him on the lips. She stepped back. "Well, big boy?"

"Why can't you ask him … he'll tell you," Morris said, his dick pressing hard in his jeans. He tried to hide the bulge with his hand and then said to her, his voice changing, "Come and finish this off and I'll think about it."

Linda walked over to him, unzipped his jeans and pulled his cock out. For someone still only 17, he was well endowed.

She left it sticking out and walked away, a wide grin on her face. She looked at him and said, "If you want that in me again, you'll do what I tell you to do, all right, Morris? Now do your jeans up and go home … its 1 o'clock and I'm shagged." She smiled wickedly.

He looked at her. "Ain't you going to finish it off for me, then?"

"Not right now matey. Now get off home. When you get something for me, you can come around again, all right."

She took his arm and walked him to the door. " 'Night, Morris."

She opened the door, pushed him out and once she had closed the door behind him she leaned back and burst out laughing.

Chapter 23

THE LAST DAY OF SEPTEMBER WAS WINDY AND VERY COLD. THE RAIN WAS BEATING DOWN SO HARD MORRIS COULD HARDLY SEE IN FRONT OF HIM AS HE WALKED ACROSS EUSTON ROAD WITH HIS DAD. IT WAS A WEDNESDAY AFTERNOON, THEY WERE GOING OVER TO THE WELLINGTON PUB IN CRAWFORD STREET TO SEE HIS UNCLE JOE, HIS DAD'S BROTHER.

Morris spoke loudly above the noise of the traffic. "Here, Dad, what does Uncle Joe want now? He ain't tapping you again, is he? Bloody cheek."

Mike Wright looked at his son. "No, he ain't and don't get bloody cheeky. He wants me to get him some meat from the Greek's place but it's a bit dodgy now as they've got new security cameras everywhere. Why, I don't bloody know."

"I know," Morris thought to himself going red in the face.

They reached the pub, both soaking wet. Mike's brother Joe was waiting for them, leaning on the bar.

He said hello to his brother and ruffled Morris's hair. "You look like a drowned rat, mate," he said with a smirk, "bloody day, ain't it?" He looked again at Morris and said to him, "Randy git … I saw you coming out of the James's house the other night. You giving that Linda one are you, or her mother?"

"No, I ain't," Morris said to him, "I just walked her home, that's all. Linda, I mean. I wouldn't touch her mother with a barge pole; she's had more pricks than a well used dartboard."

"Yeah," his Uncle Joe said to him, "so has that daughter of hers."

"Well, I ain't screwing her. Anyway, she's Jimmy Day's girl and I ain't having him chasing me about her, he's fucking mad. Nutcase, he is."

"You can say that again, boy," Morris's dad said. "Anyway, Joe, I can get you a couple of carcasses of beef and a sheep. I've worked it with the lorry driver to bring 'em out. You want 'em? 50 quid."

"Great, Mike … tell him Thursday night. Usual place. Thanks. Want another drink … and here … I'll give you the 50 now. I'll cut the meat up myself and sell it on the knocker to the locals again. They snapped my hand off before for it."

Morris looked at his dad. "You got any spare cash, Dad, for me? I'm potless."

"Here," his Uncle Joe said giving him a £10 note, "take your girl out for a drink but watch her fella," he teased.

"Thanks, Uncle Joe," Morris said. "Look, Dad, I'm off, I'll

see you at home tonight." He looked at his Uncle Joe mouthing 'thanks again' and walked out into the pouring rain.

* * *

Leo Stern was in his office overlooking Arsenal's Highbury Stadium. His minder, Tommy, was sat in a chair at the back of the office reading a comic ... or trying to. He couldn't read or write but liked to pretend he could. Leo looked at him, thinking to himself, "Thick as two short planks but handy to have around." He then decided to share his thoughts with Tommy. "What you think about that Jimmy Day, Tommy?" He stood up and walked over to the big window. Leo could see footballers training on the pitch across the way. He hated football ... but only because he couldn't get his bribes into the players.

"Well, boss," Tommy said, "he's only 17 and he's dangerous and he's going to get stronger as he gets older. He's also got a lot of youngsters around him, too, who are also getting older and wiser and, as I've been told, dedicated to him come rain or shine, so it might be in your best interests to get rid of him. Know what I mean, boss?"

"Yeah, Tommy, you've got the right idea. I'll have to think about that, even though I don't like to get too involved with killings and all that, but with Jimmy boy it's a different kettle of fish. You're right in saying he's dangerous, because he's young. If I let him get the better of me, they'll all try it on."

Leo's cast his mind back to when he started out in protection, drugs, vice and all the rest. It was over 20 years ago.

He'd had to fight for North London like a tiger. "Just 'cause I'm short don't mean I can't get heavy as well," he used to say to his victims as he slashed them across the face or back or buttocks, whatever took his fancy.

He had met Tommy ten years ago in a nightclub he had owned. Tommy had been hired as a doorman and he was good, bloody good. He wasn't scared of anyone. Leo used him to the limit. He would do anything Leo told him.

"Well, Day is doing what I asked so far. He's paying us every Friday, ain't missed yet … I can't put my finger on it but something feels wrong. I can feel something is going to happen, but what?"

Tommy got up from his chair and put his comic on the desk. He walked over to Leo, put an arm on his boss's shoulder and said, "Don't worry, boss, he ain't going to bother you. He's making enough money at the moment and he's only trodden on your toes once. He's a bit wary at the moment I think, don't worry."

"Yeah, you're probably right. But if he comes on too strong, I'll have to get rid of him."

He looked up at Tommy. "There's talk that he put that black drug-dealer away a couple of months ago. What you think?"

"Na, shouldn't think so. Looked like a hit to me, boss. I don't think the kid is into drug-dealing anyway. It wouldn't serve his purpose to kill that guy."

"I think I'll forget about him for the moment, Tommy … just keep getting the dough off him every week. Come on, let's go and eat."

* * *

Morris was just about to go into the fish and chip shop when a voice called out, "Hey, Morris, hold up a minute."

He looked round and saw Bertie on the other side of the road. "Oh shit," he murmured, "what the fuck does he want? … Hi, Bertie, what you doing?" Morris said, standing under the canopy so he wouldn't get wet.

Bertie ran over the road and stood beside him. "Hello, mate, where you been lately? Jimmy's looking for you."

"What … I ain't done nothing …" he said, a worried look on his face.

Bertie looked at him bemused. "Didn't say you had done anything, Morris. He wants to ask you about them Asians the other night."

Morris looked relieved. "Oh," he said, "where is he?"

"Over in Jack's Cafe. Come on, get your fish later."

They ran across the street and down the small alley where Jack's Cafe was. As they entered, Morris spotted Jimmy at the far end. "God, he's got that stupid coat on again. He must go to bed in it," he thought.

"Hello, Morris," Jimmy said to him as they came across to his table. "Where you been then? Sit down." He shouted across to the man behind the counter. "Jack, two Cokes, and give me another bacon sarnie."

Morris sat down opposite Jimmy. "He looks fucking bigger," he thought to himself.

"Just like to thank you for phoning the other night, Morris. Nice one. I owe you for that."

"Think nothing of it … that's what mates are for," Morris said, feeling braver. "Got anything planned at all … anything you can involve me in, Jimmy?"

"Yeah, something coming up soon, mate … I'll keep you informed. Don't worry, by the way."

"Uh oh, here we go," Morris thought.

"You heard anything about that job we did at your dad's work the other month?" Jimmy said.

"Nothing, Jimmy," he replied, feeling relieved. "My dad's back to nicking meat again. Anyway, as you said before, the Greeks ain't going to say anything, are they? They must think the money was nicked on the ship going over there, so that's that, and they ain't going to use the same scam again, are they, Jimmy?"

Jimmy looked at him and, speaking softly, said, "If you get any more scams like that, Morris, you let me know, won't you? You'll be well paid, all right?"

"Right, Jimmy. Look, I've got to go, get the old man's fish. He's over in The Wellington in Crawford Street with my Uncle Joe. You know him, lazy bastard, never worked in his bloody life. Anyway, I've got to cook his bloody tea for him. My dad, I mean. I'll see you around, all right?" Morris pushed his chair back, got up, said goodbye to them and walked out of the cafe.

Bertie watched him go out then turned back to Jimmy and said, "I don't trust him, mate. I wouldn't tell him anything at all."

"Don't worry, mate, I've got him covered. Come on, I'll buy you a pint over at The George. Let's go."

* * *

Morris Wright got his dad's fish and went back to his flat as fast as he could, muttering to himself as he ran through the pouring rain.

"I thought that bastard Day had me fingered. Shit, I'll have to be careful with that bloody scrubber Linda."

Chapter 24

MICKY WAS TAKING THE PISS OUT OF THE DRIVER AS THEY GOT ON THE BUS TO THE WEST END.

"Any more of your bloody cheek, boy, and you're off. That goes for the rest of you, too," he said, looking at the others as they got on.

"Yeah, yeah, mister, we love you, too," they chorused as they made their way to their seats.

"Bloody kids," muttered the driver as he pulled away from the bus stop.

"We going to do a bit of steaming today, Jimmy?" Paul asked him. "Might do, mate, but a lot of cops are around this time of day. Lets get things sorted out first. I want to get some rings off that jewellery shop in Regent Street first."

"Cor thats going to cost you mate," Paul said to him. "That shop's expensive."

"Dozy bleeder" Bertie said taking his baseball cap off and hitting Paul on the head with it. "We're not going in there to buy we're not spending, we're going to nick the rings."

The bus pulled up near Oxford Circus just after 10.30am. The gang all ran for the door, swearing at the driver.

"Up yours, arsehole," Pete White shouted.

"You want some of this, bastard?" Sammy Jones yelled as he got off.

"Get a life, driver," said Jackie Sweeney.

Bertie punched the side of the bus. Jimmy Day kicked it, saying, "Fucking idiot."

The bus pulled away. The driver looked at them, shaking his head, and stuck two fingers up in the air. "And up yours," he mouthed at them.

"Come on, you lot, into McDonald's. Bit of breakfast first then a bit of thieving later," Jimmy said.

"How we gonna do that, Jimmy?" Sammy Jones asked him as they walked back up Regent Street and into McDonald's.

Jimmy looked at him. "Look, mate," he said as he put his arm around his shoulder, "I'll tell you the plan inside while we're having a nosh, all right?"

"Right, Jimmy," Sammy said, walking up to the counter to order his burger.

When they were all sitting down and eating, Jimmy started to tell them his plan to rob the jewellery shop.

"Right, when we go out I'm going to buy a bit of chewing gum and when I …"

"What you want gum for, mate?" Pete said.

"Will you shut up and bloody listen to what he's telling you,

Dumbo?" Bertie said to him, kicking out angrily at his leg.

"Fuck … what you do that for?" Looney said, bending down to rub his shin.

"Are you finished, you two? If you are, I'll get on with it. So, I'll get the gum, make it nice and sticky. Right, when I go into the shop, I'll ask the girl behind the counter if I can look at some rings. They usually give you a tray to look at. I'll tell her I'm getting engaged."

Micky Taret interrupted. "But, Jimmy, don't you always take the girl with you when you buy the ring? I mean, she likes to pick her own ring, don't she?"

"Good point, Micky, I'm glad one of us is taking interest," Jimmy said, looking at the others. "Bertie, tell them will ya. I'm going to get another burger." He got up and walked over to the counter, shaking his head.

"Now bloody listen. Me and Jimmy planned this last week with a girl we know, Jenny Smith. You lot don't know her, she's from out of town. One of our extra vices. She's on the game for Jimmy."

"Wow," Paul White said, "didn't know you were into that."

"We're into a lot of things you best not know about yet," Bertie said. "Anyway, Jenny is meeting us outside the shop at" … he looked at his watch, "12 and … "

Jimmy sat down again and looked at Bertie. "Right, I'll carry on. When I meet Jenny we'll go into the shop posing as boy and girlfriend."

"You ain't wearing your long coat and cap, Jimmy, are you?" Micky said to him. "They will suss you out right away."

"Do you think I'm daft?" Jimmy said, standing up. He took

his cap off, giving it to Bertie. He then took off his long coat. "What you think of this, then?"

Under his coat Jimmy had put on a smart blue cotton jacket with a shirt and tie and white soft cotton trousers. "Like it?" he asked, giving them a twirl.

"Smart, Jimmy," Micky said.

"Cool, man," Paul White said, shaking his hand.

"Way out, man," Sammy chuckled.

The rest cheered and clapped. "All right, all right, let's get back to business" Jimmy said. "When me and Jenny are in the shop, she will ask to see a tray of rings. When she gets them Bertie, here, who will be in the corner of the shop, will trip over and fall on a display of polish they advertise in there for cleaning silver. It's there every week piled up, about 50 tins of it. Anyway, when he falls over, everyone will look over at the noise … I got the idea from a movie I saw," he paused. "I will then nick a couple of rings off the tray, put them into the chewing gum and stick them under the counter. I'll be that quick no-one will see me, then I'll tell the girl we'll come back later and collect the ring that Jenny wants." He paused again and then spoke, "Then we'll wait outside until the girl who showed us the rings goes out to lunch, then Jenny will go back in and get the rings from under the counter after asking to look at some watches or something."

"Hang on, hang on," Jackie said, "why don't you nick the rings and stick them in your pocket in the first place?"

"Well, brain box, I'll tell you. Just inside the shop there are two cameras and they'd see me pocket the rings but not see me sticking them under the counter, and if they suspected us

186

of doing the lifting, I don't mind them searching me or Jenny 'cause we ain't got nothing on us, have we? Know what I mean?" Jimmy said smiling.

"Fucking brilliant, Jimmy," Sammy said getting up and shaking his hand, "bloody brill."

The others showed their approval, shaking his hand and clapping him on the back.

Jimmy looked at his gang, his chest puffing up. He felt great, powerful. "Nothing will stop me from getting what I want," he said to himself. "Come on, let's go, Bertie. You lot stay across the road from the shop. Don't stay together and be ready if I need you. Let's go."

They filed out into Regent Street, pushing past people, knocking the hats off others, pulling up girls' skirts and then swearing at taxi drivers as they hooted at them.

"Fucking hooligans," one of them shouted at them as he drove past.

Finally, they reached the store opposite the jeweller's.

"Right, hang about and don't club together. Move about," Jimmy said to them.

He looked across the road and saw Jenny waiting. He turned to Bertie. "Right, off you go, get in the shop, I won't be long."

When Bertie crossed the road and disappeared into the shop, Jimmy crossed Regent Street, walked up to Jenny and kissed her on the lips. He smiled at her and said, "Have to make it look real. Come on, let's get it on."

Chapter 25

THE RING THEFT WENT WELL. JIMMY WALKED OUT OF
THE JEWELLER'S WITH JENNY HANGING ON HIS ARM.
THEY CROSSED THE ROAD, IGNORING HIS GANG, WHO
WERE ALL HANGING AROUND THE BUS STOP OUTSIDE
BURBERRY'S.

Bertie, who had followed them out of the shop, followed the
couple across the road. Jimmy headed along Regent Street
and cut down Maddox Street, turning into St George's Street
and up into Hanover Square.

He then walked into the small park and sat down with Jenny
on one of the many wooden benches and waited for his gang.

"Wow, Jimmy, that went well, didn't it?" Jenny said to him.
"How you manage it beats me," she smiled at him.

Jimmy stretched his legs before replying, and said, "Yeah,
pretty good, wasn't it?" He put his hand into his pocket and

withdrew the chewing gum which was in two rolled up balls and very sticky.

"Yuk," he said, splitting one of the balls of gum. He pulled out one of the rings he had stolen, threw the gum away and did the same with the other. He wiped the rings clean with his handkerchief, put them both into the palm of his hand and said to Jenny, who was looking at them in amazement ,"Over 5,000 there, Jenny. Not bad for five minutes work." He smiled. "Look, how much you got for me this week, Jenny? You had a good week?"

"Not bad, Jimmy," she said, opening her handbag and pulling out an envelope. Jenny passed it to him, "800 in there for you," she said to him.

"No, you keep it, Jenny and tell Tess to keep hers, you've earned it. Listen, don't mention it to the others, just between me and you. Now off you go, I'll see you later. Here, don't forget your money," he said passing it back to her.

She gave him a kiss on the cheek and walked away, just as his gang came into the park.

Bertie sat down next to Jimmy. "All right, mate," he said, "made a right bloody noise, them tins, didn't they?" They both laughed. "And that manager … what did he say?"

"Sorry, Sir", he said, "are you OK, Sir?" He wouldn't say that if he knew that we were robbing him." He looked at Jimmy again. "How much … you checked them yet?"

"Yeah, I have, about five grand, so we should get one or two for them. Lenny's brother is going to have them."

"How d'you know they're worth that much Jimmy?" Bertie asked.

"Yeah, you know about jewellery then, mate?" Jackie Sweeney added.

"I know nothing about them rings at all. It's just that me, Lenny and his brother Quiff – he was called Quiff because he loved listening to Bill Haley – went down to look at them rings last week. Quiff knows his gems, don't worry. Used to work for a jeweller years ago. Keeps tabs on the trade by buying stolen gear. Anyway, his wife Val was with us and she looked at them while Quiff put a value on them for us, that's how I know."

He looked at his gang. "Any more questions?" he said, trying not to laugh. "You all sound like that bastard Sergeant Sanders." He stood up, took his long coat and baseball cap off Bertie and put them on.

"Here, Jimmy" Pete said to him, "can I hold them there rings a minute?"

Jimmy laughed. "Leave it out, Pete," he said, "all it needs is for some smart alec to see us looking at them and put two and two together and call the Old Bill. I'll let you look at them later before I get rid, OK? Anyway, let's piss off … I've got to meet Quiff and Lenny at 2.00 and it's 1.30 now. Let's blow … and don't get into any bother on the way back to our manor. We don't need any cops around us with this gear on me, right?" He looked at them, waiting.

They all nodded. Paul turned to Jimmy and said, "Why don't we get a cab?"

"Fuck off," Bertie said to him, "are you thick or something? There's seven of us, cabs only take five. Come on, let's get the bloody bus."

* * *

191

Jenny Smith sat at the bar in the old George pub, off King's Cross Station. It was her regular haunt, mostly full of drunks, pimps and petty thieves. A dive, but it suited her; they were her kind of people and she felt safe there.

It was 7.30pm and she felt a bit tipsy. Jenny had been celebrating most of the day after Jimmy had given her the 800 quid back.

Jenny had been on the game for Jimmy for just about a year with her mate Tess, who she was waiting for. Even though they were only 17, they were very street-wise and knew that one of Jimmy's other mates was always close in case of trouble with a punter.

"Watcha, sweetie," a voice said to her. Jenny turned to see her mate Tess standing behind her. Jenny slipped off the stool and gave Tess a hug.

"Hello, lovely, where you been? I've been here since 6." "Sorry, Jen, I had a punter up in a hotel round the corner. Wanted me to tie him up and parade around in a school uniform. I tied him up all right. Took his money and fucked off." They both burst out laughing.

"Is he still there?" Jenny asked.

"Yeah, he is. I'll phone the hotel and let them know he's still in the room. He won't be able to pay by cash though, I nicked it all." They both cracked up with laughter.

"Here, forgot to tell you. Jimmy Day said I have to tell you, keep all your earnings for the week," Jenny said to her, smiling.

"Cor, ain't that nice of him? I spend all the week with me legs open and I didn't have to do it after all," she said laughing again. "Thanks, Jimmy boy."

Tess looked at her mate. "You know, I don't like him much, even though I work the streets for him, the bastard."

"Yeah, I know Tess, but he's all right sometimes ain't he?" Jenny said, her speech slurring a little.

"I know, Jenny, it's funny really. He screwed us both and put us both on the game the next day. Great guy, ain't he?" She grabbed hold of her mate's hand and said, "Come on, Jenny, let's go clubbing and forget about fucking blokes for one night. What you say, hey?"

"No, let's do better than that. I'm fed up being here in this bloody squalor night after night. Let's piss off to France. We've both got passports and money. One of the girls I used to know lives down on the south coast and she tells me they love young English girls over there." She looked at her mate and said, "What you say then, Tess?"

Tess grabbed her friend's hand. "Jimmy will fucking kill us for this, you know that, don't you? We won't be able to come back here, that's for sure, but bollocks to him." She pulled Jenny off the stool. "Let's do it, mate, come on."

* * *

Quiff gave Jimmy £1,500 for the rings. "And that's pretty good, Jimmy," he said to him as he paid over the money.

"I know, Quiff, and thanks."

Jimmy, Bertie, Lenny and Quiff were all sat in Lenny's old caravan in his scrapyard, smoking and having a beer. The rest of the gang had dispersed.

"We'll meet up later down the club, OK? I'll give you your

cut then," he had said to them.

"How much you giving them, Jimmy?" Lenny asked. "They didn't really do much, did they?"

"Fifty quid each should do it, I think, don't you, mate?" Jimmy said to Bertie.

"Yeah, that's enough, they only kept watch. And me, mate, how much?" he laughed.

"Five hundred for you, my mate," Jimmy said, slapping him on the back. "You did your work well," he laughed, "even though you nearly brought in half of Regent Street with the noise."

He looked round. "Well, let's go and have something to eat and then nip down the club and pay the boys."

Chapter 26

"MORNING, SARGE," ROWLEY SAID TO HIS PARTNER AS HE WALKED INTO THE OFFICE THEY SHARED. "NICE DAY, PISSING DOWN AGAIN ... HOPE WE AIN'T GOING OUT IN IT."

Sergeant Sanders looked at his young partner and thought to himself, "Bit of a plonker, but he'll make a good copper eventually."

"Yes, we are going out in it, so keep your coat on and bring them special gloves. The boys in blue found a body over in the canal this morning. Young man, they don't know if it's foul play." Sanders stood up and walked over to get his overcoat.

"Where did they find it, Sarge ... round here?" Rowley asked.

Sanders looked at him and said, "No – over in Crennon Street, back of King's Cross Station. You know, off York Way."

"Oh yeah, I know, where the old brewery used to be. Ain't they got a new boozer near there, Sarge?"

"Yes. Anyway, you ready?" he asked, looking at his partner.

"Right, Sarge". Rowley opened the door and stepped followed by Sanders.

As they made there way to their car, Sanders said to him, "You heard anything from your snitch on Jimmy Day and his mob yet, John?"

Rowley was fastening his safety belt as Sanders looked across at him, waiting for a reply.

"Nothing at all yet, Sarge, but he will slip up eventually, believe me."

"I wish I could believe you, John. I've got a gut feeling that something will happen soon. Let's get over to the canal and look at this body they've dragged out. You never know, it might be Jimmy Day." He laughed to himself.

* * *

Jimmy's dad, Tommy, lay stretched out on the bed of his lover, May Bell. Her flat was next to Tommy's and they'd been lovers for over six years, even when his wife had been around.

May came into the bedroom carrying a bottle of beer. "Here, lover boy," she said, handing him the beer and sitting down on the bed. She was dressed in a voluminous woolly dressing gown which made her look older than her 44 years. May was quite pretty, with a nice figure which was starting to bulge. "I'll have to stop the bingeing Tommy, I'm getting fat," she kept saying to him.

Tommy never listened. He was always boozing and watching TV, but she loved him and wouldn't keep pestering him for help.

"Hey, Tommy, you ought to slap that son of yours. He called me an old tart yesterday," she said, nudging him in the ribs. "Are you listening to me or what?"

Tommy put the bottle down on the side of the bed. He sat up straight, leaned over to May and gave her a kiss on the cheek. "Look, sweetheart, my son Jimmy doesn't think a lot of me. We are gradually getting together again and if you think I'm going to have a go at him, think again … and anyway, he's young, 6ft, bigger and fitter than me. You want me, a 56 year-old drunken fart, to have a go at him? Forget it."

He picked up his beer again, looked at her and said, "Sorry, love, no chance."

"You fucking weakling," she screamed at him, "your son calls me a whore and you do nothing."

"You're a whore, are you? No, you're not, so forget about it. It's just talk … he's still angry with me and he's taking it out on you, OK?"

He got up and walked around the bed, pulling her up. "He'll come around, believe me. Come on, get your togs on, I'll treat you to fish and chips. Come on, hurry up." He pulled her to him and kissed her on the lips. "Don't worry, OK?"

* * *

Thursday night was a busy night in the Nag's Head, always a lively pub, frequented mostly by Irish. It was the day of the week when most of the labourers got paid. It was early evening and Jimmy Day was sitting at the bar talking to Lizzie the barmaid.

"Your son still living in the States, Lizzie?" he asked her. She used to be a mate of Jimmy's mum's and he used to talk to her a lot. Bit of advice here and there. Jimmy thought she was a real gem.

"Yeah, he's doing fine, Jimmy. He phoned me last night, goes to Stamford University in February. Nearly 19 you know, miss him terrible."

She felt a bit sorry for him, even though she knew he was a right little bastard … but she liked him. "Going over when me and Eric get some money saved up. Ain't seen him since he left two years ago. Anyway, never mind, he's well, that's the main thing."

"You're a good mum, Lizzie. My mum used to tell me about the little things you and Eric did for her and my brother and me. I'm eternally grateful, and while I remember," he put his hand inside his jacket pocket and withdrew a small package. "This is for you, a little present from me and Mark." He looked at her, seeing the surprise in her eyes. "And I don't want it back, all right? Now go away and serve someone. Morris Wright's just come in and I've got to have a word with him." He slid off the barstool and walked over to Morris in the other bar.

"Hi Jimmy, what's new?" Morris asked as Jimmy approached.

"Watcha, Morris, what you say? How's your dad, all right?"

"Yeah, thanks Jimmy." He laughed. "Still has no idea about

that scam you pulled. Pity is, you can't do it again as I've heard the old man telling my uncle they do it another way now."

"Never mind … so what's the score, Morris, what you up to nowadays?"

"Nothing, Jimmy, not a lot about. Not very many scams I can get into. You got anything coming up?" he asked.

"Well, still got my protection going on the shops. Me and Bert also do a bit of collecting debts for some people over South London. They ask us to do it 'cause no-one knows us over there, so if we do a bit of slapping around it can't be traced back to the lenders." He looked at Morris. "Get it?" he said.

"Sure, Jimmy," Morris said, not really following him.

"Anyway," Jimmy said "I've got something coming up soon, couple of weeks, I think. Might be able to fit you in, all right Morris?"

"Great, mate, what's it about anyway? Something local, I hope?"

"It's about that little shit Leo Stern … I'm going to hit that big bastard he calls a minder."

"Bloody hell, Jimmy. He's big-time, you mess with him and he'll have your balls for cufflinks. I'm telling you, he's bad news."

"Let me worry about that, mate." Jimmy had already had a few drinks and was beginning to open up. "That bastard don't worry me, I'll fucking have him, you see."

"When you going to hit him Jimmy. Soon?" Morris asked. The more you get from him, the more you can screw me – Linda's words had made a significant impact on Morris

199

"I'll let you know, Morris. Anyway, I'm going back into the other bar. Got to meet Bertie and the rest of the lads in there. Look, come in Friday, I'll be in here for a while. We're all going up West dancing, bit of thieving as well. You want to come with us?" He looked at him, waiting for a reply.

"Might do, Jimmy. I'll have a drink with you all, at least," Morris said.

Jimmy drank the last of his beer and put his glass down. He put his hand into his jeans pocket, took out a wad of £10 notes, peeled two off and threw them down on the counter. "Here, get yourself a drink." He walked out and into the next bar.

"Cor, fucking hell," Morris said, picking the money up and stuffing the top pocket of his not-so-trendy jacket.

He picked up his unfinished drink and downed it in one. He got off his stool, looked through to the other bar, checked that Jimmy couldn't see him and walked over to the phone. He dialled the number he had written down, waited and then spoke. "Hi, can I speak to Linda, please? Tell her it's Morris."

Chapter 27

FRIDAY NIGHT AT THE NAG'S HEAD WAS THE SAME AS
ANY OTHER NIGHT, JIMMY THOUGHT TO HIMSELF AS
HE LOOKED AROUND THE LARGE BAR ROOM. THE ONLY
DIFFERENCE WAS, ON A FRIDAY NIGHT YOU GOT ALL
THE OFFICE STAFF IN, SO IT WAS NOT AS EASY TO GET
A QUICK DRINK, EVEN IF YOU WERE A LOCAL. A TUG
AT HIS ARM MADE JIMMY TURN. IT WAS HIS BROTHER
MARK.

"What you drinking, bruv? Can I have one?" Mark asked
him.

"No, you bloody can't, you can have a shandy. Lizzie!" he
shouted, "Give my brother a shandy, half only," he laughed.
"Don't want him passing out on me," he said to her as she
came across with the drink.

"I want a word with you, young man," she said to Jimmy.

"Come over here." She beckoned him over to the end of the bar.

"Wait there, Mark, keep your eyes open for Bertie and the rest of the boys." Jimmy looked at the clock above the bar. It was just on 8pm. He looked at his brother and said, "They should be here in a minute. Just having a word with Lizzie." He walked over to the corner of the bar where Lizzie was waiting for him.

"What's up love?" he said to her, putting his arms on the bar. "Someone upset you?"

"Yeah, you have. I can't take this money, Jimmy. Three grand, bloody hell. Where you get three grand from? You steal it or what?" She looked at him, a tear forming in the corner of her eye. "You're a lovely bloke, Jimmy, even though people say you're no good … but to me you're OK, but I can't take it. Where you get it from?"

Jimmy looked at her. "Look Lizzie, I'll tell you. I found a briefcase a few months ago up on the top deck of a bus up West. Didn't know what was in it. Look, I took it home with me. My dad opened it with a knife". He looked at her, the lies forming more easily.

"He cut around the lock and when it came open there was all these bundle of notes inside."

"Why didn't you hand it to the local police then?" she asked, wanting to believe him.

"Do me a favour, love," he said, "the cops would have kept the money. They're all bleeding bent, they would nick their mum's handbag if they could. Anyway, that money I gave you, it was for what you did for us when my mum died. It's yours,

I don't want it." He looked at her. "Go and see your son, Lizzie, it might be your only chance. Please."

"Why not?" she said. "You're right, them cops would have kept it. You be careful, Jimmy, and a thousand thanks, but what am I going to tell the old man? Can't just come home with three grand, can I?"

"You still go to Bingo, don't you, Lizzie? Say you won it. I'll get a couple of the married women who owe me a favour to back you up. Know what I mean, Lizzie?"

"You are a one, Jimmy Day, but I'll never forget you for it. Thanks a million. I've got to get back serving. That old bastard will give me the sack seeing me chatting all night. See you later, Jimmy." She pointed over to the far door. "Your mates have just come in ... you take it easy and take care of your brother," and she walked away to serve a punter.

* * *

Morris Wright was trying to get Linda's skirt up. They'd been walking over by the canal which ran alongside Regent's Park. Linda had said to him, "It's better if we got out of the way in case one of Jimmy's mates sees us."

They had stopped under the canal bridge where Morris had pushed Linda up against the dirty damp wall.

"Come on, Lin, you promised me a good time if I gave you some info on Jimmy."

He lifted her skirt to the top of her legs and was trying to get his fingers into her knickers. He could feel her wetness as he found her vagina.

203

"Come on baby, let me in," he said pulling his zip down with his other hand. His penis was rock solid as he struggled to get it out.

"You fucking wait," Linda said to him, pushing his hand away from her. "How do I know what you told me is true? You could be just saying that to screw me again."

"No, no, it's true Linda, honest." Morris was stroking himself, desperate for some action. "Oh shit," he cried, as he came all over his hand and Linda's skirt.

"You dirty bastard, look what you've done. It's all over my fucking skirt. My mum will kill me if she sees this. I'm going home. Up yours, Morris Wright."

She wiped herself down with a handkerchief, but even though it was dark she could see all the stains. "Jesus," she said as she walked away from him.

Morris zipped himself up and ran after her. "Sorry, Linda," he said, catching her up. "I'll walk you home. A few dodgy characters around here."

She looked at him, stony-faced, and said, "Yeah, and one of 'em is walking beside me. Listen, Morris, I need a bit more than what you gave me on Jimmy Day. You get it, and I'll do anything you want all right?"

She looked at him, thinking what a tosser he was if he thought he was going to screw me again. Not a bloody chance.

"Come on, then, Lin I'll take you to your door and I'll try and get more for you." Morris was finding walking alongside Linda a little painful … he'd caught his dick in his zip.

* * *

Jimmy and his gang were in the Zoom Room, a club off Brewer Street in Soho. It was a club mostly for the younger crowd, and was owned by Lenny's brother, Quiff.

"It's the young 'uns who have all the money," Quiff had said to Lenny the day before it opened. "Nobody over 21 gets into this club." Quiff had about ten girls working for him, a couple of Swedes, some Russians and three Italians. The young blokes loved 'em.

Bertie and Jimmy were sitting with two of them. Russian Nina was with Jimmy. She was big and busty. Bertie was with Letty, who was Swedish.

"Some birds, ain't they, Jimmy?" Bertie leaned across and said into his mate's ear. "Hope they let us screw 'em tonight."

Jackie Todd was leaning over the table talking to Paul White, who was celebrating his sixteenth birthday. "Look at them two," he said, pointing to Jimmy and Bertie. "Them two scrubbers will suck them in and blow them out in bubbles." They both laughed. Jackie continued, "I feel a bit pissed ... what about you, Paul?"

Paul looked at his mate, sweat pouring down his face, and wiped his forehead. "Yeah, I feel a bit funny, but I think it's all this bloody smoke in here."

A noise at the club door grabbed the crowd's attention. A couple of blokes were trying to push their way into the club. Quiff and one of his doormen were trying to push them back, with no luck.

"We want to come in, matey. Come on, honest, no trouble," one of them said, trying to push Quiff away.

"No fucking chance, mate, you can't come in. Its under 21s only in here."

"Yeah, them women look more like bloody 41," the bigger man said, looking over at Jimmy's table. He took a swing at Quiff, hitting him on the chin. Quiff fell backwards on to the floor, banging his hand.

Jimmy jumped up off his seat, saying to Bertie, "Come on, mate, Quiff needs a hand out there," as they ran across the small dance floor. Jimmy pulled his flick-knife from his pocket. He reached the door as the two men pushed the doorman out of the way.

Jimmy raised the knife as the first man came down the small steps that led into the club. He whipped the blade across the man's face, causing a deep cut from his lip to his ear.

The man screamed, putting his hands to his face. Jimmy kicked him in the balls. The man went down screaming. Jimmy turned to the other man who just stood there. He said to Jimmy, putting his hands up, "Not me, mate. No trouble, let me get my mate, please, and we're out of here."

Jimmy looked at him, the anger boiling over in him. Bertie came up behind him, looked at his mate, then at the other man standing in the doorway and said to him, "You better get your mate and get out while you have the chance and don't come back."

The man nodded, walked down the steps, put his hands under his mate's arms and pulled him up. He looked at Jimmy and then at his friend, the blood pouring down his face, and dripping on the floor making a small puddle.

"You didn't have to cut, him, mate … we would have gone out."

"Fuck off while you have the chance," Bertie said to him, "and get your mate to a doctor."

As the man helped his pal out of the door, Bertie turned to Jimmy. "Wow, mate, you didn't have to cut him, they would have gone."

"I don't think so … you see the way he punched Quiff? My way was the only way." Jimmy wiped his knife on a tissue and dropped it back into his pocket.

He turned round to his gang. "You're supposed to fucking help me in punch-ups, not watch," he glared at them. Jimmy walked over to Quiff who was still down on the dance floor. He helped him up. "You all right, Quiff? Sorry about that, but he asked for it."

Quiff looked at him. "Thanks, Jimmy, bit strong, the cutting, wasn't it?" He dusted himself down looking around at the people who were still quiet.

"Drinks on the house, folks, and let's have some fucking music." He turned to Jimmy and said, putting his arm around him. "You better stay out of here for a couple of weeks, mate, in case the cops come sniffing, all right? I can't see them blokes saying anything, but just to be safe … know what I mean, Jimmy?" He patted him on the back. "Come on, let's get you a drink and get that bird to give you a good time."

They walked over to the girls' table where Nina and Letty were waiting. Bertie was already sitting next to them. The girls looked really scared. Quiff looked at them, smiling, "Come on, girls, let's have a smile." He looked at the Russian. "Right, Nina, you give Jimmy a good time tonight, OK?"

The tall girl stood up and walked over to Jimmy. She looked

at him with contempt, saying, "I wouldn't touch you with a barge pole, Jimmy Day, you're a fucking maniac." She looked at Letty. "Come on, Letty, let's get out of this madhouse."

Jimmy looked at the women as they walked out of the club. He looked at Quiff, shrugged his shoulders, laughed and said, "Fuck 'em."

Chapter 28

ARAN PATEL AND HIS BROTHER AHMED WERE SAT IN
THEIR COUSIN'S SHOP IN DRUMMOND STREET, OFF
EUSTON ROAD.

"You know, Beddal, I saw that bastard Jimmy Day this
morning. He had all his gang with him as usual. When you
going to do him, cousin?" He looked at him, waiting for a reply.
When he didn't get an answer, he stood up and walked over to
the small counter, opened a fridge at the back of it, took out a
cold bottle of water, unscrewed the top and drank the contents
straight down.

Wiping his mouth with the back of his hand, he turned to his
cousin again. "Well, you gonna answer me or what?"

Beddal Mistry looked across the small shop at Aran. Slowly,
he raised the stump of his arm up where his hand used to be
and said angrily, "Oh, I'm going to get him all right, don't worry

about that. We're going in Friday night. Your mates backing us still, Ahmed?

"Yeah, we have about 30 guys with you lot, I should think. That will be about 50 … plenty I think, don't you, Aran?" He looked at his brother, who was now trying to open a Mars bar.

"Yeah, that will be enough for them bastards. They'll run like jack-rabbits, believe me, cousin."

It was just after 8.30am on Monday morning. The rain was pouring down. Aran looked out of the shop window, cursing. "Where's that bloody girl? I wanna open the shop but I can't unless she comes in." He looked at his cousins. "My dad won't let me do the shop by myself," he said, shrugging his shoulders. "Where is she?"

As he finished speaking, the bell on the shop door rang once. Beddal got up and walked over to the door. He unlocked it and opened it wide. He looked at the girl outside, the rain pouring off her shoulders. Paula Young looked back at him, drenched. "Sorry I'm late, Beddal, the bus was late. Is your dad in yet?"

"Come in, come in. No he ain't … I've got to go soon, you manage on your own until Dad comes in," Beddal replied. "Go and dry yourself in the back, then you can open the shop."

"Thanks," Paula said, and walked into the shop and through into the back room.

"Bleeding little scrubber," Aran said to Beddal, "I don't know why your dad keeps her on."

Beddal looked at his cousin. "There's nothing wrong with her … she's quite a good worker and, anyway, Dad likes her."

Ahmed looked at his brother and cousin. "What we doing about Jimmy Day, then … is it on Friday night or what?" he asked.

Paula Young listened intently from the back room,

overhearing the plans that the Asian boys were discussing. She finished drying her hair, brushed it, put on the apron and walked back into the shop. Glancing at the boys, she said to Beddal, "You can all go now, I'm ready to open up."

"Thanks Paula, see you later," Beddal said to her. He looked at his cousins. "Come on, let's go. See you, Paula," and he walked out of the shop.

* * *

Jimmy Day picked up the phone as he walked into the front room. He cradled it on his shoulder while he lit a cigarette.

"Yeah, who is it?" he said, blowing smoke into the mouthpiece, "is that you, Bertie?"

"No, it's me, Jimmy, Paula Young, at the Paki shop."

"Hi, Paula, what you want, sweet? Bit early, ain't you, it's only 9.30 … need some help, babe?"

"No, no, Jimmy, its them Paki boys, heard them talking in the shop this morning … they're coming to get you, Jimmy."

He sat up, transferring the phone to his hand. "What do you mean, Paula, they're coming to get me?" He laughed, "I'm really worried."

"Don't laugh, Jimmy, they mean business. About 50 of them, Friday night. They're going to get you and the boys as you come out of the pub, but it's you they want, Jimmy, big time."

"Look Paula, I … "

"Listen, Jimmy, I ain't got time, let me finish. That Beddal wants your arm, Jimmy. He says he's going to cut it off and he bloody means it, too. I've got to go now, Jimmy."

"Thanks, Paula, I owe you. What time they coming, did they say?"

211

He could hear her breathing down the phone. "11 o'clock, Jimmy. Be careful." The phone went dead.

Jimmy sat looking at the phone in his hand. "Thanks, Paula, thanks," he said to himself as he replaced the receiver. He picked it up again and dialled Bertie's number. While waiting for him to answer, Jimmy said to himself, "I'll fucking swing for that Paki."

"Hello, hello, who's that?" Bertie's Irish brogue rang out. "Is that you, Da?"

"No, it bleeding ain't, it's me, Jimmy. What you doing?"

"Nothing, mate, it's pissing down with rain. You doing anything, Jimmy?"

"No, not yet. Listen to what I've just heard." Jimmy went on to tell Bertie about Paula's phone call. When he'd finished Bertie, butted in.

"You believe her, mate, do you think she really heard all that?"

"Yeah, Bertie, I do. She's never let me down yet, she's OK."

"What we gonna do then, Jimmy? Take 'em on Friday night or what?"

"You fucking bet, mate. Look, phone up some of the boys and get 'em over here. I'll get hold of Morris."

"What you want him for? He's fucking useless, Jimmy."

"I know, I know, Bertie, but he can get a load of weapons off his uncle for us, that's why I want him here. I use him, get it?"

"Right, Jimmy. Look, I'll be over in 20 minutes." Bertie put the phone down.

Jimmy looked at the phone in his hand. "Cheeky bastard, I ain't finished talking yet," and he laughed as he put it down.

He got up out of the chair and walked through the living

room door, and up to his brother's bedroom. He opened the door and looked in. Mark was lying on his stomach, snoring very loudly.

Jimmy closed the door quickly and went to his own bedroom. He quickly got changed, had a wash in the bathroom and went back down to the living room. He looked at his watch; it was 10.30am. Jimmy sat down, lit another cigarette, picked up the phone again and dialled.

He waited for an answer. "Hello, Mrs Neil, is Dancer in? It's Jimmy Day."

"Hello, Jimmy, ain't heard from you for a while," Mrs Neil said. "Yeah, he's here. Hang on."

"Watcha, Jimmy," Dancer Neil said to him. "What you after?"

"Got a big punch-up coming Friday night with the Pakis. You interested, Dancer? About 50 of 'em."

"You bet I'm interested, mate … you want some of the boys over there to lend a hand?"

Jimmy had met Dancer a couple of years ago on the Tube station one Saturday night down the West End. He and the boys had been to a disco. They'd heard a commotion down the other end of the platform and ran over to see a white kid (Dancer) getting a kicking from five Pakistani youths. Jimmy had steamed into them with his gang and soon had them on the run.

Dancer had never forgotten Jimmy and the boys and they'd been mates ever since. If Jimmy ever needed help from Dancer and his mates, he got it.

"Yeah, mate, I might need you. Can you get over Friday night?"

"'Course I'll be there. I'll get the boys together, maybe about 20 or so. With your gang and some of their mates, should be enough. I'll go round to some of my mates' houses today, see if they're all right for Friday. I'll get back to you on Thursday night, OK?"

"Right, Dancer, I'll wait for your call later in the week then. I can give you more details then. You know the time, the place and so on. See you later, Dancer, stay cool."

Jimmy put the phone down, stood up, and walked into the small hallway. He opened the front door and walked out on to the balcony to wait for his mate Bertie.

He didn't have to wait long. Bertie appeared at the other end of the balcony, shuffling along, looking knackered. He came up to Jimmy, sweat pouring off his brow.

"Bloody lift, out again. I must have lost a bloody stone in weight climbing them stairs. What's happening, Jimmy?" Bertie looked at him, waiting for a reply.

"Hi, mate, come on. Let's go inside. Got a lot to tell you."

They both walked back into the flat, going straight into the living room. Bertie sat down in the armchair. Jimmy sat at the table.

"Well, Jimmy, what's the score? We up and ready for them Pakis or what?"

"You bet, mate." Jimmy stood up, walking round the table. He spoke excitedly. "I've got Dancer and his boys coming over Friday night. Maybe about 50 of 'em. With our lot, that should do, I think, don't you?"

"Yeah, Jimmy, we should breeze it." Bertie looked at his mate, not so sure of himself. "How we gonna get them this time, mate?" Bertie asked, a worried look on his face.

"Well, mate," Jimmy said to him, "it's going to be like this. There's a disco over at the King's Head near York Way. You know, the old pub. Anyway, opposite the pub you've got the old warehouse on one side, on the other is the … "

" … old brick wall," Bertie finished the sentence for him. "I get it, mate. We'll be waiting over the wall and in the old warehouse for them bastards … nice one, Jimmy, nice one."

"Not quite," Jimmy said. "A couple of things you missed out, mate."

"Such as?" Bertie said.

"For one … and don't interrupt this time," Jimmy said, "all of us won't be at the fight. Lenny, Gummy and Jackie will be high-tailing it down to the Paki shop in Drummond Street about 11. They'll torch the shop, burning it to the ground, I hope. They they'll come back here to finish off the fight with us later when we've done the Pakis.

"You, me, and Micky the Ferret will go over to the camera shop in Tottenham Court Road and burn that bastard down as well." He looked at Bertie, his chest swelling with pride. "Any questions, mate?"

Bertie looked at his hero. "Yeah, a few, Jimmy. One; how are you going to get to the camera shop from the pub? That's if we come off best in the fight."

"We will, believe me, mate," Jimmy said.

Bertie carried on, "And the other thing, what about the weapons? What we gonna use?"

"Right, mate. First, Lenny's coming with us to the shop so he'll take and bring us back. There's a little square at the back of Tottenham Court Road where he can park and get away fast. The other thing, Bertie, is we're going to use chains, baseball bats and cabbage knives … will that do for you?"

"What the fuck are cabbage knives?" Bertie asked laughing.

"Well, my son, they're bloody 15in knives used to cut cabbages. It's what the hicks use on the farms. I've got 20 of 'em. Cost me a hundred quid … and you know what hicks are, don't you?"

"Yeah, they're people who chew straw and live 20 miles out of London. Essex and beyond," he went on.

They both burst out laughing. Bertie added through his laughter, "How can you tell if you screwed an Essex girl?"

"Don't know, how do you?" Jimmy said.

Bertie rolled off the chair in fits of laughter. "Straw on the end of your dick," he said.

Jimmy had to sit down he was laughing so much.

"Come on, let's get on with it," Jimmy said when they'd controlled themselves. "You phoned the boys like I asked you, Bertie?"

"Of course, they should be here soon." Bertie looked at Jimmy. "I don't know why you asked that Morris round, I don't trust him. Did you know he's still screwing that Linda?"

Jimmy laughed, looking at his mate. "I use him, mate, like I used her. Who gives a shit about him? But he comes in handy, know what I mean?"

As Bertie was about to answer, the doorbell rang.

"Must be the boys," Jimmy said. "Let 'em in, mate. Look, Bertie, don't worry about Morris Wright. He don't know nothing important. He can't hurt us and, anyway, why should he? The only thing he knows is about me meeting Leo on Saturday. He knows nothing about money or anything."

Jimmy lit a cigarette and sat down again. "Let 'em in, Bertie."

Chapter 29

WEDNESDAY MORNING WAS COLD AND DAMP AS LINDA JAMES AND HER MATE SHEILA HIGGS WALKED DOWN EUSTON ROAD TOWARDS KING'S CROSS.

"Are you sure you're doing the right thing, Linda?" Sheila asked her. "If Jimmy Day finds out you're grassing him up to the Old Bill, you're bleeding dead and me as well," she said, her eyes showing her fear.

"Don't worry about it, Sheila. How's he gonna know? You gonna tell him?"

"No I bleeding ain't," Sheila glared at her friend. "What you take me for?"

"Don't get your knickers in a twist, I'm only joking," Linda said, "and, anyway, the bastard deserves it after what he did to me. Come on."

They stopped at the bus stop and jumped on a No 6 as it stopped.

Linda grabbed hold of her mate's arm as they boarded the bus. "Come on, Sheila, let's sit downstairs," and pulled her over to the seats near the ticket collector's area.

Linda sat down first, her short skirt riding up to the top of her legs, showing her knickers. The conductor took their money and gave them their tickets. He then sat down opposite them, looking at Linda's legs.

She looked at him with a sneer, saying, "Had a fucking good eyeful, you dirty pervert? I'll have the cops on you." The conductor looked away as everyone looked at him. He stood up, his face crimson red with embarrassment and walked up the steps to the top deck.

"What you do that for, Linda? You love it when blokes look at you and, anyway, you wear them skirts so exactly that."

"Yeah, I know. Anyway, here's our stop. Come on, the cop shop's just over there. Now what's that bloody cop's name again? Sergeant Sanders, that's it." They both jumped off the bus as it pulled in to their stop.

As the bus drove off, the conductor put his middle finger up in the air, mouthing to them, "Up yours."

"Cheeky bastard," Sheila said giggling. "I know what he'd like to do to you, mate."

"Yeah, don't I know it. Lets go," she said, as they walked across the road and into the police station.

* * *

Jack Todd was about 50 yards away from the bus stop on the other side of the road as Linda and Sheila got off the bus and walked across the road and into the police station.

Jackie was with his younger brother Jake. They were going to the Mount Pleasant post office to collect a parcel for their mum.

"Now, I wonder what them two are doing going into the nick?" Jack said to his brother.

"Might have been caught on the game," Jake said to him, laughing. Jake was only 12 but knew everything that went on. "Or," he went on, "she might be grassing someone up … and look who's with her, that old slapper, Sheila Higgs."

"Yeah, yeah, come on, Jake, let's go. I'll give Jimmy a ring later, see if he knows anything about it. Let's go and get that bloody parcel."

* * *

Sergeant Sanders and Detective Rowley were sat in the charge room reading a report on the body that had been found in the canal a week before.

"An old dosser, Ken, I think. Can't find anything out about him at all," Sanders was saying to his partner.

"Looks like it, Sarge. Poor old bastard." He looked at his boss. "You want a coffee, Sarge? I'm going over to the shop to get a sandwich."

Sanders looked at his partner, thinking to himself, "That's all these young coppers think about, bloody eating, drinking and screwing. God help us."

"Just get me a coffee and hurry up, we're out at 1. Got to see Chief Inspector Glenn … he wants to see us about that inquiry into David Smith's death."

"Is this going all the way then, Sarge," Rowley asked him,

looking worried. "If they suspend us, we're in big trouble, ain't we?"

"Don't bloody worry, John, we'll be OK. Just don't lose your head. Anyway, what they going to do? Glenn ain't got nothing that will stand up to an inquiry … Go and get them coffees."

Rowley got up, walked over to the door, opened it and walked out. A minute later, he was back sticking his head round the door.

"Sarge, got two young ladies out here. Want to see you." He smiled. "About Jimmy Day!"

Sanders jumped up, nearly knocking his chair over.

"Blimey," he said, "send them in, send them in and, John, get two more coffees."

Rowley closed the door behind him as he went out again.

Ken Sanders put two chairs in front of his desk, went around it and sat down again to wait for his unexpected visitors.

Fifteen minutes later, John Rowley ushered the two girls in, both of them holding coffees. John Rowley was holding the other drinks but no sandwiches.

Sanders stood up holding his hand out to the girls.

"Hello, I'm Sergeant Sanders, CID. Is there something I can do for you?"

Linda James held her hand out. "Hi, I'm Linda James and this is my best mate Sheila Higgs."

Sheila nodded to him. "Hello," she said.

"Well, sit down, girls," Sanders said, pointing to the chairs.

When they were settled, he looked at them. "Well, what is it you want to see me about?"

"Well," Linda said, "it's about Jimmy Day." She looked at her mate.

"Go on, go on, don't be frightened. Anything you tell us won't leave this room," Sanders reassured them. "Ain't that right, Detective?" He looked at his partner.

"That's right, Linda," he said, "whatever you tell us about Jimmy won't get out of here, so just tell us what you know." He smiled at the girls, thinking to himself, "What a pair we have here. I bet the whole bloody street has been through these two."

Linda crossed her legs, giving John Rowley a quick flash of thigh, and said, "Well, Inspector ..."

"Sergeant, Linda ... I haven't been promoted yet."

"Well, Sergeant, Jimmy Day has got a big meeting on Saturday night with Leo Stern." She looked at both of the policeman. "I'm sure you know who he is."

Rowley looked at Sanders, smiling. He said, "Oh, we know him all right. Go on."

"Well, Jimmy's going to meet Stern at Pancras Way at 5.30. It's about a protection racket Jimmy's been running. He's been stepping on Leo's turf so Leo is making Jimmy pay him every week."

Sanders looked at her. "How do you know all this, Linda, and why are you telling us?"

Sheila spoke up. "Jimmy had her gang-banged one night at a party at his flat. His whole gang raped her."

Rowley looked at Linda, his smile vanishing. "Look, Linda, we can arrest him for that right now, just give us a statement and I'll get a warrant for him."

"Not on your bloody life, mate. My life won't mean a bloody thing then ... or my mum's. You've got to be kidding.

Sanders looked at Linda and said, "Look, Linda, I know

that Day is a right bastard and I aim to nail him and, with your help, we will. If you don't want to give evidence against him about the rape, don't, but … " he looked at her, "give us as much as you can. Whatever you have, tell us, OK?"

She looked at him, wishing she hadn't come now. She felt a bit frightened. "This is a different kettle of fish," she thought to herself. "I … I … " she hesitated. "I think he murdered that black man down the arches weeks ago. Jimmy was bragging to me one night about it. Said he smashed his head in with a lump of wood 'cause the black man was selling drugs to kids."

Sanders smiled at his partner, "Got him, John, bloody got him."

"Hang on, hang on a minute, I ain't bleeding making a statement about that. No chance, mate." Linda started to get up.

"Sit down, Linda, sit down," Sanders said to her. "You don't have to give evidence if you don't want to." He bent down behind the desk and reappeared with a tape recorder. "I've got it all down here what you told me. I'll get it all on this, don't worry. Anything else you can tell me?" he asked. "What about the Asian fight when that kid lost his hand, anything about that? You heard anything?"

"No, nothing," Linda said, even though she was there when Jimmy had done the Asian. "And if I did, I ain't saying no more." She got up, and said to Sheila, "Come on, let's go."

Sanders stood up as well. "Look, Linda, what you said about Leo Stern, it ain't much. Nothing at all. If you have anything on Jimmy Day, give it to me while you're here."

"Come on, Sheila, we've been here too long."

Sheila got up and followed Linda to the door, which Rowley

had opened for them. He smiled at them. "Thanks for coming in," he said.

Linda stopped and turned round to look at Sanders. With a sullen look on her face, she said to him, "I've also heard Jimmy's plotting to kill Leo. Don't ask me when." She turned again and walked out of the room.

* * *

When they had gone, Detective Rowley came back into the room. He looked at his boss. "What you think, Sarge?" he said.

"Don't know, but we're going to be there. Too bloody right, I'm going to arrest him on that rape allegation, anyway. That will give us a boost, but not yet."

"What you mean, Sarge? Let him roast, till Saturday?"

"Yeah, that's it. Get the bloody lot of them together." Sanders laughed. "I've been waiting for this and, at last, I think I've got him."

He got up, looked at his watch and walked over to John Rowley slapping him on the shoulder. "I'll buy you a drink to celebrate and then I'll tell you what I want you to do. Come on."

Chapter 30

FRIDAY WAS A DULL, MISTY MORNING, LIGHT RAIN FELL AS BEDDAL MISTRY WALKED ACROSS DRUMMOND STREET AND INTO HIS DAD'S SHOP. IT WAS 9.30AM. THE SHOP FELT COLD AND DAMP AND THE SMELL OF SPICES MADE HIM FEEL A BIT SICK. HE CLOSED THE DOOR BEHIND HIM, THE BELL ABOVE THE BADLY HUNG DOOR RINGING AS IT CAUGHT THE THIN METAL STRIP ALONGSIDE IT. HE LOOKED ACROSS AT THE SMALL COUNTER IN THE CORNER OF THE SHOP. HE SHOUTED, "DAD, DAD, YOU IN THERE?" THE STORE ROOM DOOR OPENED, BUT IT WAS PAULA YOUNG WHO CAME OUT.

She smiled. "Hi, Beddal, your dad's gone out, won't be back until midday. Did you want him for something?"

"No, it's just that I've got some family coming over today for a wedding, I'm sure my dad's forgot."

"No, he ain't, that's why he's gone out, he's going to order some stuff for the wedding." She shrugged her shoulders. "That's what he told me, anyway."

"Has Aran been in yet?" he asked.

"No, he phoned though, about five minutes before you came in." She smiled again. "Don't worry, I wrote the message down for you, it's over there, near the phone."

Beddal walked over to the phone and picked up the notepad on which the message was written. "Thanks, Paula," he said to her, "don't know what we would do without you. I'll see you later, things to do … " then he walked over to the door, opened it and left. Paula waited until she was sure he had gone, then went to the phone. She dialled a number.

"Jimmy, it's me, Paula … listen, the Asian boys are coming over at 11 tonight, about 50 of them. Yeah, that's right, Jimmy, you take care, I'll see you later." She put the phone down as a customer came in. "Hello, can I help you?" she said, smiling.

* * *

"It's on, mate," Jimmy called out to Bertie as he put the phone down.

"Great, who was that? Paula?"

"Yeah, and if it weren't for her, we would be in trouble. Now let's get it worked out for tonight." He looked at Bertie. "What time we all meeting up with the rest, Bertie?"

"9. They're all coming at 9, mate. I booked the hall at the King's Head. It's ours until 2am, Jimmy."

"How many we got coming?" Jimmy asked.

"About 100, mate. Your pal from over the river is bringing some and Old Shaggy Black is bringing a few." Bertie looked at Jimmy, laughing. "How did he get a name like that?"

Jimmy, laughing, got up. He walked over to the cabinet, took two beers out, passed one over to Bertie and said, "He likes screwing older women, mate, you know, about 40 to 50, and he's only 17 - the dirty bastard."

They both laughed.

"I want our boys with us when we go at the Asians, Bertie," Jimmy said, a violent tone in his voice. "I want 'em round me, our own gang."

"Right, Jimmy … you want me to start getting organised, phone the lads up, you know, and your mates over the water?"

"No, I've already arranged that with them. They'll be in the King's Head at 8.00 tonight. I think Shaggy will be over at 9, so it only leaves us to get hold of our lot and make sure they're ready."

"OK, mate … now what about Lenny? Is he coming with us or what?"

Jimmy got up, walked over to the sideboard and picked up another beer. He looked at Bertie and said, "Want one?"

"Yeah, please, mate," Bertie said. Jimmy threw him a can. "Here," he said, "when you've finished, make tracks and get us organised and, yeah, Lenny is meeting us at the pub at 8.30. I've got a few things to do, then I'll catch you later, all right?"

Bertie got up, walked over to Jimmy and slapped the palm of his hand on to Jimmy's saying, "Let's get it on." He picked up his coat and walked out of the room, followed by Jimmy. They walked out on to the balcony. "Still bloody raining,"

Jimmy said. "Mind you, if it rains tonight, it might be an advantage." He patted Bertie on the back. "Right, mate, I'll see you tonight. Oh and, by the way, wear our gear tonight. Tell the boys if we happen to get done, it will be nice to go out in our colours. See you later."

* * *

Sergeant Sanders looked at Rowley. "Look at this," he said, waving the letter in front of him.

"What is it, Sarge?" his partner asked him with a worried look on his face.

"We are on suspension from Monday. Shit! I don't believe it."

"What … what you saying?" John Rowley sat down heavily. "It can't be. Why? Why?"

"Over young Smith's death. The Chief wants someone's head and it looks like it's going to be ours."

Rowley thought to himself, "Not me, mate, I'm not losing my career over this." He spoke up. "What does it mean, Sarge?"

Sanders said, "It means, laddie, that after next week we'll most probably not be coppers any more."

Rowley turned white. "You've got to be kidding. You said that they ain't got nothing on you."

"On us, laddie, on us, and don't forget it. Anyway, this weekend we are going to make the bust of our lives. I don't think they'll want to dump us then," he smiled, "do you?"

Rowley looked at him, thinking to himself, "What a right bastard you really are." He spoke, hiding his anger. "No, I don't, Sarge. I bloody hope not. This will kill my mum and dad if it comes to that."

Sanders walked over to the young policeman, put his hand on his shoulder and said, "Don't worry, mate, this thing tomorrow will get us in the clear, so put it out of your mind. Right you got everything sorted for tomorrow?"

"Yes, Sarge, all the men have been briefed and we've got two gun permits off the judge. Hope that we won't want them, though."

"Right, laddie. Get off home with you and I'll meet you tomorrow at the pre-arranged place, OK, and don't worry about a thing. Now off with you."

* * *

Drummond Street was buzzing. There was a wedding going on. The Asians shops were decorated in traditional regalia. Beddal looked at his cousin Aran. He spoke with no trace of fear in his voice. "You got everything sorted out for tonight, Aran?"

"You bet, cousin, the boys are all ready, we're going in about 10. I've got information that they're all going to the King's Head, hired a hall at the back of it."

"How many have they got, do you think?"

"Not a lot … they don't even know we're going to have a go at them tonight, so they'll be caught unawares. I reckon there will only be about 20 of them. We'll give them a right kicking, cousin, don't worry."

Beddal spoke again. "Jimmy Day is mine, don't forget that, and tell that to the others, right?"

"Right, Beddal, don't worry, he's yours, believe me."

* * *

Mark looked at Jimmy. "So he's taking me over to Brighton for the weekend, Jimmy. Peter, her husband, is taking us down this afternoon. Why don't you come with us, bruv? It will be nice."

Jimmy looked at his brother. "Na, I can't, Mark, I've got a lot to do over the weekend. You go and have a nice time." He put his hand in his pocket and pulled out a wad of bank notes. "Here," he said, passing over three £20 notes, "bring me back a lobster."

Mark took the money, stuffing it into his pocket. "Thanks, Jimmy. Right, that taxi should be here in a minute." He put his coat on and picked up his small suitcase. "No need to walk down with me, the cab will take me to the hotel where they're staying. I'll see you Sunday night. Any message for sis?"

"Na, tell her I'll see her on Sunday … she can take me out to dinner." He gave his brother a hug and walked him to the door.

The flat seemed cold and damp when Mark had left. Jimmy's dad was away as well, having gone to Liverpool with his fancy piece and he wasn't back until Monday. Jimmy looked at his watch; it was just after 4. Time to have a bath and get changed. He wanted to be out for about 6, he had a lot to do and not a lot of time to do it in.

* * *

It was still raining as Jimmy walked into the King's Head. It was packed to the rafters.

"Hi, Jimmy." Dancer walked across to him and patted him on the shoulder. "You want a drink, mate?"

Dancer looked Jimmy up and down. "Wow, you look cool, like your long coat. Nice hat. I see all your boys have them on."

"Yeah, mate, it's a special night for us. I wanted us all to look the same, it puts the fear into people when you all look the same." He put his arm around Dancer's shoulders. "I'll have a beer, mate, thanks. All your mates in, Dancer?"

"Bet your life, Jimmy, they're all here. Brought over only 20 though … some of them couldn't make it. Should be enough with your lot and Shaggy's mob."

Jimmy looked at him. "Yeah, that's right, I don't think we'll have to worry about the Pakis, they'll only be expecting about 30 or 40 of us. Anyway, let's have a look, see who's here and sort things out for later. He looked at his watch, it was just after 8.30pm.

They walked out of the bar and into the private hall at the back of the pub. As they entered the hall, a big cheer went up. Jimmy looked around, seeing all his mates and their friends. Jimmy called Bertie over.

"Right, mate, get someone on the door, no one in, no one out until I've finished, OK?"

"You've got it." Bertie looked at him. "All ready for it, then?"

"You bet, mate … get the door."

When he saw the door guarded, Jimmy stood up on a table, his long coat swirling out as he put his hands up for silence.

"OK," he addressed them as best as he could, "you know why we're all here and I'm grateful to you all for coming over here to help. You've all got your instructions from your main men, but just to refresh your memory … "

They all looked at him in awe. Hardly any of them knew him, but his reputation was known over most of London, despite his age. He was respected by young and some old villains alike. He went on, knowing he had their attention.

"Shaggy, you take your lot over to the far side of the road. Wait behind the wall there until I give the nod. Leave here about 10.00-10.30. Got your clubs and things?"

Shaggy nodded, and he looked up at Jimmy, smiling. "All ready, Jimmy, whenever you say go, we go." He turned around to his gang. "Right, boys?"

A big cheer went up from all around. "Up 'em, Jimmy!" "Kill the bastards!" "Send 'em back!"

Jimmy put his arms up in the air for silence. "OK, OK, boys." He looked at Dancer, then at his own gang. "You know what to do." He nodded to Dancer. "You come over when Shaggy goes in to get them … you'll have them completely by surprise. Right, any questions?" He looked around.

A dead silence spread across the room, then he heard a giggle by one of the girls who was sitting down below Jimmy's table. Jimmy glared at her. She looked away, turning bright red.

"OK then, so be ready when I tell you. Until then, have a drink and a good time. Let's make sure these bastards never come back to our manor." He jumped down amid cheers and walked back to the makeshift bar at the back of the room.

Bertie came over and patted him on the back. "Nice speech, Jimmy." His own gang - Micky, Jackie, Paul, Lenny and Pete - soon surrounded him. He looked at them all, laughing, and said, "Right, mates, this might be the last big punch-up for a while. Make the most of it. Have a drink on me."

* * *

The Asian gang were caught completely by suprise, like lambs to the slaughter. They were ambushed from all sides. Aran, Beddal's cousin, was so badly beaten he lost an eye. But some of Shaggy's gang were slashed across the face, and some of them had broken limbs, as did some of the Asian boys.

Jimmy Day came face to face with Beddal. They hit each other with baseball bats until Bertie hit the Asian on the back of the head, knocking him out. Jimmy and Bertie then gave him a terrible kicking, breaking his ribs and stamping on his face. Some boys on both sides were so badly beaten it took six ambulances to ferry them away.

The police arrived too late to stop the fight. Nobody was arrested out of the 150 gang members who had been fighting. No one had seen a thing!

At the right moment, Jimmy and some of his gang managed to get away. They burnt down not one, but two Asian shops, as well as the camera shop in Tottenham Court Road. As they made their way home in Lenny's van, Jimmy, still bleeding from a cut over his eye, looked at his mates and said with a smile, "What a night. Them Pakis won't be back and that pervert won't be selling pornos any more." He looked at Lenny. "Come round tomorrow with Bertie. Just that scumbag to deal with and North London is ours."

Chapter 31

THE RAIN WAS COMING DOWN HEAVILY, THE WIND SLASHING THE RAINDROPS INTO THE WINDOW OF JIMMY DAY'S BEDROOM. THE STORM OF THE PREVIOUS NIGHT WAS STILL RAGING, EVEN NOW IT WAS 10.30 ON SATURDAY MORNING.

Jimmy was sitting on the edge of his bed. He had pulled a chair under his legs so he could write. The letter was to his brother Mark. He always wanted to tell his brother the things that he was doing, and why he always had money ... but he couldn't bring himself to tell him; he didn't want Mark to turn out like him.

Jimmy finished the letter, putting it into an envelope. He wrote on it "For my brother Mark".

He pushed the chair back from his legs and stood up, walked over to the window and peered out.

"Jesus, what a day," he said to himself. "Hope it bloody clears before this afternoon." He turned and walked back over to the bed, threw the letter on it, bent down and pulled out his old box from underneath. He unlocked it, took the key back out and put it in the envelope.

Jimmy opened the box and looked down at the contents. On top was his baseball cap. He took it out and laid it on the bed; next, he took his long black coat out and laid it next to the cap. At the bottom of the box lay photos of his mum, Mark, Alison and himself taken years ago. He picked up a photo of his mum and murmured to himself, "Hi, Mum, sure miss you." He put it back on top of the other photos.

Other items in the box included valuables he had stolen up West – rings, watches, neck chains snatched from around women's necks, cameras from tourists and so on.

"All yours, Mark," he said out loud.

Jimmy was meeting Leo Stern and his bodyguard later at the back of the old postal depot in Pancras Way at 5.30pm, and he knew he wouldn't be home today, and probably for a very long time – if ever – because of what he planned to do.

He laid the coat back in the box, put the cap on top and closed the lid. He put the padlock back on and clicked it shut, pushed the box back under the bed and stood up.

He picked the letter up and walked over to the far wall near the door. Hanging on the wall opposite his bed was a full-size cut-out of Kim Basinger, which he had nicked one night from a cinema up the West End. At the back of the figure, Jimmy used to leave his money in a pocket he had made, and he also left money for Mark or a message for him.

His dad never knew about it and, anyway, he never went in

Jimmy's room. Jimmy slipped the letter into the pocket and walked back to the other side of his bed where his wardrobe stood. He opened it and looked inside. It was packed with clothes he had bought over the last couple of years. They would all fit his brother, eventually.

He selected an old pair of Levi's, a polo shirt and an old Burberry wax jacket which he had lifted out of a car a couple of years ago in Harley Street, where all the old quacks had their private practices, and other things Jimmy could mention.

He carried the jeans and polo shirt with him and walked out of the bedroom and into the bathroom. The flat was empty, deadly quiet. Mark had gone out with Alison and her husband for the weekend. "Jimmy couldn't make it," Mark had told his sister, who was down for the weekend. "He'll see you when you get back, all right?"

"He'd better," she had said to him.

He finished washing, dressed and came out of the bathroom. He walked into the kitchen and put the kettle on. On top of the tea caddie was a message from Mark which was a day old. It read: "Can I wear your sloppy Nike sweatshirt, Jimmy? If so, can you leave it out for me? Love, Mark."

Jimmy laughed. "You can have it all from tonight, I think," he said to himself.

He made some toast, put the milk in his tea, stirred it and carried it over to the table. He was just about to sit down when the phone rang.

"Shit!" he said getting up. He looked at his watch; time had flown. It was now after midday.

"Blimey, that went quick." He walked over to the living room and picked up the phone. "Hello," he said, "who's that?"

"It's me, Jimmy, Jackie Todd. I thought I'd phone you to tell ... "

"Hello, Jackie, what's up?" Jimmy asked, interrupting him, "you sound out of breath, mate."

"Yeah, listen, Jimmy. I saw Linda James going in the King's Cross nick on Wednesday. I was going up to Mount Pleasant with my brother and we saw her with her mate, that old slapper Sheila Higgs."

"Thanks, Sweeney, but I wouldn't worry about it. She ain't got nothing on us mate. Most probably lost her knickers. Thanks, anyway. See you later, Jackie, and thanks again." Jimmy put the phone down and went back into the kitchen to finish his breakfast.

Jimmy was waiting for Big Lenny and Bertie to come up. They were going with him to meet Leo. "Just to be on the safe side, Jimmy," Lenny had said to him the night before, when they had burned down the Asian shops and the camera shop in Tottenham Court Road. The camera shop owner had refused to give Jimmy any more money, so Lenny, Jimmy and some of the boys had gone back after midnight and put petrol through his letter box. "The shop must be badly gutted," Lenny had said later, "we put enough bloody petrol in it."

Jimmy knew there would be trouble today when he met Leo to give him his money, and that's exactly what Jimmy wanted. The bell on the front door made him jump. He got up and walked to the front door.

"Watcha, Jimmy." Big Lenny stood there with a wide grin on his face. Bertie stood behind him.

"Hi, Jimmy ... thought you were going to phone me this morning, in case anything happened about last night."

"Na, that pervert ain't going to say nothing. He'll tell Leo but not the cops, but Leo won't have time to do anything, believe me. Come in, anyway."

They stepped into the flat, and made for the kitchen.

"Sit down … want a beer?" Jimmy asked them.

"I'll have one," Lenny said.

"Not for me, Jimmy, thanks." Bertie looked at him. "Lenny's got your stuff." He lifted a bag up. "I've got that false arm for you, but what do you want it for?"

"I'll tell you. Sit down, sit down." He waited for them to sit.

"Look, I'm going to put that arm in my right-hand sleeve just like a proper arm, then I'm going to put a bandage and a sling on it, you know, so it looks like I've fractured my arm or something. My real arm is going to be inside my coat, my hand holding that long needle Lenny's got for me." He looked at Lenny. "You did bring it, mate, with the other thing?"

"Yes, 'course I did." He opened the box he'd been carrying. He took out the needle which he handed to Jimmy.

Jimmy looked at it. "Wow, done a good job, mate." The needle was pointed like a sword and was pushed into a cork with metal on the bottom to stop it going all the way through. The needle was about 7in long. Jimmy thrust it in front of him, testing it, like a sword.

"Great, got the acid as well?"

"Here." Lenny took a slim bottle out of the box. It was covered in tape. Jimmy lent across the table and gently took the bottle from Lenny.

"The tape is to stop it slipping out of your hand," Lenny said. "What you want it for?"

"I'm just getting to that, mate. Right, when Bertie and me walk up to Leo and his goon, I'll put my left hand into my pocket and take out the package of money. Leo will think it's money, but it will be paper. As I pass it to him, he'll come up close to me. As he takes the package, I'll grab his arm, pull him towards me and stab him with the needle which will come out of my coat at exactly the same time as I pull him to me." Jimmy looked at Bertie. "Bertie, as I hand him the package, you throw that acid into the goon's face. You've got to do it at the same time as the handover. You understand me?"

His mate looked at him, a bit startled at his friend's description of what he wanted him to do. He frowned and said, "I don't know if I can do it Jimmy. I might … "

Jimmy didn't let him finish. "Look, mate, you have been with me all through. Don't let me down. If we don't do this, that bastard is going to get us anyway. You know what I mean?"

Bertie looked at his friend and at Lenny.

"You can do it," Lenny said to him. "Anyway," he went on, "I'll be around with something up my sleeve, so don't worry, and the other guys will be hidden and tooled up."

Jimmy looked at Bertie. "All right, mate?"

"Yeah, don't worry, Jimmy, I'll do it," Bertie replied, still frowning.

"That Asian kid's dad must have had a surprise when he went to open his shop this morning," Lenny said, laughing.

"Yeah," said Bertie, giggling. "He won't bloody find one!" He couldn't stop laughing. "We not only gave him and his pals a fucking good hiding, but a good torching, too, hey, Jimmy?"

"Some night, wasn't it?" Jimmy said looking at them both. "Look," he said, "if anything goes wrong today, get away as best you can. That bastard Leo only wants me, you know. He knows I'm a thorn in his side. He'll try to do me in."

"'Course, he won't, mate," Lenny said. "I'll be there watching your back and so will the others," he said looking at Bertie, "ain't that right, pal?"

"Sure is," Bertie said. "We won't let you down."

"I know, I know, mates, but just get away if anything happens, OK? Promise me that, right?" He looked at his two mates.

"OK, mate, we hear you," Lenny said.

"Right then," Jimmy said, "let's get on with this bloody arm."

Chapter 32

"HELP ME WITH THIS BLOODY ARM LENNY."

Jimmy had his wax jacket on and his false arm in place, but every time he lifted the arm up it kept falling down.

"Hang on, Jimmy, look, don't move." Lenny took the sling, put it around Jimmy's neck and up and over the false limb. He bandaged the false arm, stood back and admired his handiwork.

"How's that, mate?" he asked Jimmy.

"Great Lenny," Jimmy smiled. "Now just do the stud buttons up but leave the two middle studs open; that's where my hand is coming out with the needle."

Lenny did what Jimmy had told him. When he'd finished, he stepped back and said, "Right, now try it." He stepped up to Jimmy. Jimmy's hand shot out and hit Lenny in the chest without the needle in it.

"Brilliant, Jimmy," Lenny said. Bertie patted his mate on the back. "Great, Jimmy, I never saw your hand, it came out so fast."

"Just do your bit, mate and we're home and dry."

"I'll do it, mate, don't worry."

Lenny looked at the kitchen clock. "It's getting on, pal. We'll have to get off soon. The lads should be all in their places now."

"That package on the table is for you, Lenny. There's a grand in there for you."

"Thanks, mate. You ready, Bertie?"

"Yeah. Jimmy, can I have a small whisky? It will calm me down."

"Yeah, help yourself. Get me and Lenny one, too."

When Bertie came back with the drinks, they all toasted themselves. "Let's do it right," Jimmy said to both of them and drank his whisky straight down.

The rain was still beating down as they left Jimmy's flat. It bounced off their backs as they came out into the yard, 18 floors below.

"What a bloody Saturday this is going to be," Lenny said.

"No, this could be an advantage to us," Jimmy replied. "If Leo has got his goon to hold an umbrella for him, and I know he will, that's one arm we don't have to worry about."

"Yeah, you're right, Jimmy," Lenny said, "never thought of that," he said, smiling.

* * *

Sanders and Rowley were stationed under a tree behind a

small wall in Pancras Way. The girl had been right. Something was happening, and it looked big. They had watched the young gang come into Pancras Way one by one. He knew most of them - Pete Higgins, Jackie Sweeney, Micky Taret (whom Sanders had picked up twice last year). Sammy Jones, whose mum was on the game. Paul White, the local kids called him Gummy, but no Bertie 'knuckles' Cooney, a hard-case at 16. Looked 18 or more. Big Lenny wasn't there yet, either, and, of course, the one he wanted most of all, the out-of-control nutter Jimmy Day.

"What you thinking, Sarge?" Rowley asked him. The rain was dripping off his nose, his raincoat already soaked.

"Not thinking, laddie, planning. Let's get it right. Make sure them other coppers are alert and ready when I say go. Keep that radio on all the time."

Sanders had brought with him ten policemen. They had been there all afternoon, not wanting to risk detection. He had spread them all over the place, in phone boxes, old post vans, some in derelict warehouses and himself and Rowley behind the wall. He looked at his watch; it was coming up to 5.20pm.

* * *

Bertie and Jimmy walked together down the road which cut into Pancras Way. Lenny had already gone ahead.

"You nervous, mate?" Jimmy said to his pal as they came into Pancras Way.

"Not now, Jimmy … I was to start with, but I've got over it. I'll do a good job, you wait and see."

"I never worry about you, Bertie, you're my best friend. I know you'll never let me down, whatever."

* * *

"Leo's car is pulling up, Sarge," John Rowley was saying to his boss, "and big Lenny's over up on that ridge … see him, Sarge?"

"Yeah, I see him. Leo and his henchman won't get out of their car until Jimmy Day turns up. Talk of the devil, here he comes, and with his sidekick. Get on the radio, make sure the men don't make a move until I tell them, right?"

"Right, Sarge." Rowley pressed his talk button and started to organise the men.

The rain was coming down heavily again and it had become quite dark all of a sudden.

* * *

"There they are, Jimmy," Bertie said to him, looking down the road at the big car in front of them. The car door opened. Tommy the goon stepped out, putting an umbrella up.

He opened the passenger door. Leo, dressed in a white mac and hat, stepped out of the car and under the umbrella.

"You ready, Bertie?" Jimmy said to his mate. "Get that bloody lid off the acid."

"I've done it, Jimmy, it's ready. Just don't walk too fast."

"Right mate, let's do it," Jimmy said. They walked towards Leo and then Jimmy stopped.

"What you doing, Jimmy?" Bertie asked, stopping alongside him.

"Let them come to us, mate," he said, his hand tightening around the cork end of the needle. He was ready. He looked across to Bertie. "Ready?"

"You bet, Jimmy, you bet."

Leo was about five yards away. He stopped and looked at Jimmy, a smirk on his face.

"Got the goods, big man?" he smiled, "you better have. Getting me out in this bloody rain. Catch my death in this," he laughed and stepped forward. As he got within a foot of Jimmy and Bertie, he put his hand out and said, "Give, boy, and it better be all there. Then we'll have a talk about last night's fire. By the way, what's wrong with your arm? Close her legs, did she?" he sniggered. Tommy never moved or smiled.

Jimmy slowly took his left hand out of his pocket, the package already in it.

"Here," he said, as Leo put his hand out to take it. Bertie took his hand out of his pocket with the acid, stepped closer to Tommy and threw the acid into his face. At the same time, Jimmy dropped the package, grabbed Leo's arm, pulled him closer and brought the needle out and drove it straight through Leo's clothing and into his chest. Leo didn't have time to react. Tommy screamed and fell to his knees. Jimmy withdrew the needle and drove it again into Leo's chest, this time piercing his heart. Leo was dead before he hit the road.

"What the fuck is happening over there, Rowley?" Sanders roared. "Quick, get the fucking men over there. Quick, quick. Jesus Christ, hurry."

Jimmy withdrew the needle again from Leo's chest, who was by now lying on the wet road. Blood was pumping like a fountain from him. Tommy was still screaming, his hands covering his face. "My eyes, my eyes …" he kept screaming.

Bertie stood there, stunned. He couldn't believe it when Jimmy walked over to Tommy, his hands covered in blood. He looked down at the big black man.

Smiling, he said to him, "Tommy, you fucking goon bastard, this is for my dad and the kicking you gave me." He put the needle in Tommy's ear and pushed. It went into the soft bone of his left ear and came out of his right ear. Tommy rolled over and died.

It all happened in the space of a couple of minutes. Jimmy grabbed hold of Bertie's arm and pointed over to the old post building. "Fuck, look … " Men were coming out of the buildings and all around them.

"Someone's grassed us up. Let's go." They both ran over to the wall on their left, not realising that Sanders and Rowley were there. Jimmy could see more people running his way but it wasn't his own gang. He knew it was the Law. As they reached the wall, two men jumped down right in front of them.

"Hello, boys," the older one said, "going somewhere?" It was Sanders, the Scotch copper who had tried to nick Jimmy before.

Without hesitation, Bertie hit him full on the chin. Sanders went down in a heap. Rowley, trying to grab Jimmy, tripped over his Sergeant. Jimmy looked at Bertie and nodded.

"Look after yourself, mate, you ain't done nothing." He jumped over the wall and ran like he had never run before. The rain was easing up, but Jimmy kept slipping.

He looked back but couldn't see anyone, but then a figure

appeared. Jimmy could just make him out. It was Sanders. Jimmy wiped the rain out of his eyes and looked in front of him. "Fuck," he shouted. He had, without realising, run on to the railway line at the back of King's Cross. He looked back again, still running. He saw three or four cops who'd now joined Sanders. They were all gaining on him.

"You didn't fucking hit him hard enough, Bertie," he said to himself. Suddenly, Jimmy stopped. Then turned around and shouted at his pursuers, "Come on, you fucking shits. Come on." Jimmy started to run again straight into the station. He crossed the railway lines and jumped up on to the platform, knocking people out of the way. He made for the iron walkway which went over to the other platforms. Once on the walkway, he glanced down. The Sergeant and his men were now coming into the covered arch of the station. Jimmy looked across and saw a door open on the far platform. He ran as fast as he could down the iron steps across the platform and in through the open doorway. Steam was coming off his clothes now. He was sweating.

Looking around, he saw a flight of steps in front of him. He made straight for them. As he got further up the stairs, he felt a cold rush of wind in his face. Soon he came to the top of the stairs, where there was a trap door. To the left was a long room. He went for the trap door, pulled the bolt back and pushed the trap door open. He climbed up through the opening and found himself on the big glass domed roof of King's Cross Station. He looked back into the room and heard voices way below. "Fuck me, they're coming up the stairs," he said to himself.

Now panicking, Jimmy looked across the roof. He could see

a church across the way. The clock was on 7, it was darker now, too. Jimmy looked over to the Camden Town area. In the distance, he could see his block of flats.

"Fucking dump," he said and started to walk slowly across the foot passage over the glass dome. He looked down into the station, the bright lights dazzling him for a moment.

He heard the hum of the helicopter before he saw it and then it came into view, the spotlight hitting him straight away.

"Don't move, stay where you are. Don't go any further," the voice from the helicopter boomed above Jimmy.

Jimmy stopped, looked up, then looked back to where he had come from. He could see the coppers coming out of the trap door. He looked up again at the helicopter, put his fingers in the air and shouted, "Come and get me, coppers."

He carried on walking. As he got half-way across the dome, Jimmy's foot slipped and he fell, crashing down on to the glass. It gave way under him. In blind panic, Jimmy grabbed hold of the first thing he could find, his hands catching an iron rod which held the glass in place. His hands curled around the rod and he tried to pull himself up.

His face was now dripping blood, cut by a piece of glass which had shot up as he fell. His hands were also badly cut, blood dripping down his arms. His legs dangled wildly. At last, he found a foothold, but he knew he couldn't hold on for long. His arms were getting tired.

A voice above him startled him. "Hello, Jimmy boy." It was Sanders. "Got you, you fucking maniac." He lay down on the roof and grabbed hold of Jimmy's collar. "Up you come, Jimmy boy. Time to give up, laddie." He tried to pull Jimmy up. As he did, Jimmy let go with one of his hands as if to let himself be hauled up. He put his other hand into the pocket of his jeans and pulled out his flick-knife. With one swift movement, he reached up and slashed the Sergeant around the face, but Sanders, despite screaming in pain, kept hold of Jimmy's collar. "You little bastard," he shouted.

Jimmy dropped the knife and, with all the strength he could muster, he reached up and grabbed Sanders' wrist. Putting all his weight on to one arm, he pulled down hard, letting his dead weight act like an anchor. "This is for David Smith, copper." He saw the terror in the Sergeant's eyes as the copper started to slip through the hole in the glass. He tried to let go of Jimmy, but it was too late. They fell together, with Sanders screaming. Jimmy was silent. They both hit the railway lines together, their bodies smashed and broken.

Jimmy Day died first, a smile on his face. The Sergeant died on his way to the hospital, still cursing to the very last.

epilogue

THE BOY UNLOCKED THE DOOR TO HIS HOME ON THE
EIGHTEENTH FLOOR OF THE BLOCK OF FLATS ON THE
VAST ESTATE. HE PUSHED THE DOOR AND WALKED IN.
THE APARTMENT WAS QUIET, NOT A SOUND CAME FROM
ANY ROOM. HE GENTLY OPENED THE DOOR WHICH LED
TO THE FRONT ROOM, AND LOOKED IN.

"Good, Dad ain't in yet," he said out loud. Looking at his
watch, he saw that it was after 1pm. "I shouldn't think he'll be
in until at least 4, anyway. It's Saturday, so he won't be in early."

He walked around the apartment, checking all the rooms.
Finally, he went into the kitchen, pulled out a stool and
carried it over to the sink. He put it down and stood on it,
stepped on to the draining board. He reached out, put his
hand above the kitchen window and found a small shelf. He
felt around until he felt the key. He retrieved it, got down, put

the stool back and walked out of the kitchen and into his brother's room. He closed the door and leant back on it, resting his head against the cold wood.

He walked over to the bed, pushed it away from the wall and lifted a section of the wallpaper up. Behind it was a small wooden door about 10in square. He inserted the key, turned it and opened the small door. He put his hand inside and took out a small metal money box. He laid the box on the floor, opened it and looked in. He lifted out the letter his brother had originally tucked behind his Kim Basinger poster for him. He opened it and started to read it again.

"Hi, bruv," it went, "by the time you read this I'll be either doing time or dead. The latter probably. Anyway, you'll know by now about what I used to do. Blackmail, protection, stealing, etc. Me and the boys. I didn't want you to know anything at all about it, as I don't want you to turn out like me."

The boy laughed to himself and said, "I knew all along, bruv, I knew all along." He carried on reading. "Anyway, take the key off the top of the kitchen window shelf. Open my secret safe which I showed you behind my bed. Yeah, you know the one Lenny put in for me. Dad don't know about it, so not a word. Anyway, the box is yours. Take it and spend it carefully. In the big box under the bed, you'll find my baseball cap, long coat, plus arm band and baseball bat. If you don't want them, throw them. You look after yourself, my little brother, don't get into trouble like me, and look after Dad. I know you love him dearly. Love you. Your bruv, Jimmy."

A couple of tears slid down his face. He wiped them away. Putting the letter back into the envelope, he opened the money box again and took out a bundle of money. He'd been doing this for nearly a year now. He counted out £50, put it in his jeans pocket and put the rest of the money back with the letter. He stood up, leant across and put the money box back into the small wall safe. He closed the door and locked it.

He pushed the bed back, went down on one knee and pulled the big box from under the bed. He opened it, took out his brother's long coat, baseball cap, bat and strong band. He pushed the box back and stood up, carrying the coat and the rest of his brother's things, and walked over to the long mirror.

He put the coat and bat on the chair next to the mirror. Rolling the band up his arm until it felt good, he worked the bat under it. He picked the coat up and put it on. Finally, he put the baseball cap on his head. He looked in the mirror.

"Looking good," he said to himself, smiling. He adjusted the cap, turned around and walked over to the door. He opened the door and said loudly, "Well, Jimmy, let's see if I'm as good as you."

Mark walked out of the apartment without looking back.